Zagwitz

~ the ~

Thingummagadgetician

By Inigo Jones
Illustrated by Julek Heller

POCKET
BOOKS

First published in Great Britain by Simon & Schuster UK Ltd, 2000
This edition first published by Pocket Books, 2001
An imprint of Simon & Schuster UK Ltd
POCKET
BOOKS A Viacom Company

5 7 9 10 8 6 4

Simon and Schuster UK Ltd
Africa House
64-78 Kingsway
London WC2B 6AH

Simon & Schuster
Australia Sydney

A CIP catalogue record for this book is available from the British Library

ISBN 0 743 44020 X

Printed and bound in Great Britain by
Cox & Wyman Ltd, Reading, Berkshire

In memory of my dad, who never saw me grow up, and if he could read this book would probably think I still haven't.

For dearest Ros, Rhiannon and Deiniol, who allowed me those precious quiet moments. And Eluned and Maurice for their support.

With special and grateful thanks to my publishing team, all of whom are thingummantasticgorical to work with.

Contents

All of a Doodah

This particular summer's night an eeriness lurked deep within the darkness. Even the high seas trembled as the ghostly galleon swiftly cast its murky spell around the world.

An icy shiver raced along Zagwitz's spine. Almost every night this diminutive figure stood alone outside his patched-up barn, gazing at the heavens and dreaming of exploring the stars.

Zag had modified an old lean-to conservatory, added it to the barn and called it his Thingking Pad. Here he planned the more intricate and detailed aspects of his work. The hayloft of the barn was now his small bedsit, and the ample area below was divided by two large wooden doors. Behind these he had secretly built his most challenging and exciting Thingummagadget to date – and one which he hoped would at last realize his dream. He had worked extraordinarily hard at this invention, often into the early hours of the morning. Now it was finished and ready for testing.

Zag could not understand why on such a beautiful, clear night he felt so uneasy. He glanced towards the backdrop of the dense woods, silhouetted against the nearly full moon. Maybe it's thoughts of ghosts and witches that are making me feel like this, he thought. "Now you really are being silly," he said out loud to himself.

Suddenly a fork of lightning flashed across the sky, catching him totally by surprise. It was so intense that for a moment Zag was blinded. More and more flashes came and went as he protected his eyes with his hands. Peering through his fingers, he stumbled into his Thingking Pad to escape the fury, but the lightning honed its way through every pane and crack in the rickety building.

Zag's heart pounded as he crouched down. He waited nervously for some kind of outcome – huge thunderbolts, an explosion, something horrible! There was not even a drop of rain or a single clap of thunder, just a weird, deathly hush. The lightning ceased, and almost immediately the eerie silence was broken by a panic-stricken owl swooping into the barn. "Zag! Zag! Where are you?"

Zag had shared the old barn with him ever since the owl had arrived from out of the blue.

"It's okay, Awoo. I'm in here," Zag called back.
Awoo flew into the Thingking Pad and perched
on the home-made desk, looking very flustered.

Standing up to his full height, which wasn't very tall, Zag dusted off his bright green fez by slapping it against his vivid red trousers. He nearly always wore his fez, feeling that it balanced up his thinning hair with his thick, bushy white beard. "Back early, aren't you? I thought you liked going out at night-time?" he teased.

"How an owl is supposed to go about his nightly business with lightning flashing all over the place, I just don't know, old chap," said Awoo, his mood changing from a state of fear to a more composed one of displeasure.

"Frightened, were you?" enquired Zag, with a mischievous twinkle in his bright blue eyes.

"What? ME? An owl frightened of the dark?"

"I meant the lightning."

"Well, I must admit . . . Anyway, I am certain I saw you crouching down."

A broad smile spread across Zag's kindly face. "Who? ME? A Thingummagadgetician?"

"It was rather a strange experience, old chap. What do you think caused it?" Awoo always liked to hear Zag's opinion, so he could pass it on to everybody else as if it was his own. This not-so-wise gentleman owl so desperately wanted to sound wise, he'd even shortened his hyphenated name from Twit-Awoo for fear of being called "Twit".

"Well, you see – Awoo" Zag picked up his half-rimmed glasses and placed them delicately on the tip of his nose – "lightning is normally caused by the interaction of positive protons, neutral neutrons and negative electrons. Rain droplets fall to earth with a positive charge. This creates a huge voltage, a big spark, and bingo, that's lightning!"

"Quite, old chap. Exactly my thinking," said Awoo, putting on his vacant, trying-to-be-wise look, while desperately trying to remember precisely what Zag had just said.

"Trouble is," continued Zag, "in this particular instance, as far as I can tell, there was no cumulonimbus."

"What! No cumni . . . uh . . . busilimo . . .?"

Zag just managed to control a fit of laughter by quickly blowing his nose into his handkerchief. "Exactly, cumulonimbus. It's a thundercloud."

"Ahem." Awoo coughed. "Quite . . . ahem, of course. Your shoulders are shaking, old chap. Are you okay?"

"Probably a delayed reaction to tonight's extraordinary happenings," replied Zag, muffling another giggle in his handkerchief. "It will be interesting to hear what the weather people have to say," he continued, getting back to safer ground for fear of offending Awoo.

Awoo decided not to pursue Zag's opinion any further. He couldn't understand what he had been told so far, let alone try to remember anything else. "Well," he sighed, "time for some shut-eye. Oh, and please try not to make too much noise."

"Sleep well, Awoo," Zag called out after him.

Ruffled feathers

Dawn was soon to break and Zag had no time to be tired. Time was short and the twins' thingummagadgetal birthday present needed to be carefully packed and wrapped. Today was their birthday and he had promised faithfully to visit them. Zag whistled and hummed away to the background music on the early morning radio programme, as he fiddled about with Lucy and William's present. A framed photograph of himself with the two of them hung on the wall above his drawing-board. Glancing at it, he chuckled to himself. "Wait until you see what I have made for you," he thought.

At that precise moment all hell was let loose.

"Can't stop! Can't stop! I CAN'T STOP!"

The dawning of a new day had been completely disrupted by Flewy, a large seagull, who was flying around in circles as low as possible and at break-neck speed, squawking his head off. He tried desperately to land on top of the lean-to roof, but did not take account of the early morning dew on the glass. With an unplanned flutter and a sprawling tap dance, finished off with a triple somersault, he plunged into the rainwater barrel below.

Flewy spluttered to the surface to find himself being stared at by an extremely disgruntled Awoo.

"Very expressive. I'll give you five point nine for creativity," the owl mocked.

"Waaark!" squawked Flewy, angered by his own embarrassment.

Awoo looked contemptuously down his stubby beak, "Well, old chap . . . stopped for a bath, I see."

The half-dazed seagull clambered out of the water barrel. He was too occupied spreading his wings and shaking off the water to notice Zag, hands on hips, leaning against the Thingking Pad doorway and looking totally bemused. Flewy wobbled on to the grass and squawked out loud towards the loft window above. "Time to wake up, time to wake up!" He gave an ear-piercing shriek: "ZAAG! It's time to wake up."

"Try cock-a-doodle-do, that should do it," taunted Awoo.

Flewy was about to give this jumped-up owl a piece of his mind, when Zag interrupted. "You'd make an excellent cockerel, if you wore a funny red hat," he said, chuckling.

"In future, Zag, old chap," said Awoo, putting on a superior tone of voice, "try inventing a silent alarm clock."

"If he did, he wouldn't hear it to wake him up, you twit," chirped Flewy.

"With lightning all night, the radio blaring, Zag banging about and NOW YOU . . . YOU . . . YOU SMELLY, OVERBLOWN SEA DUCK! I . . . I . . . am going back to sleep!" said Awoo. Feeling he had made his point, he took off in disgust and flew back into the barn.

Zag found it awkward having two good friends

who never really saw eye to eye. Flewy was very irritating at the best of times, but it wasn't easy for a seagull to retire to the heart of the country, miles from the sea. He hated nesting on cliffs and felt much safer in a tree. Whenever questioned about this, he would reply curtly, "I would have thought it blatantly obvious: trees have branches."

"See what trouble you have got me into now!" complained Flewy, as he followed Zag into the Thingking Pad.

"Sorry, old pal." Zag chuckled. "Anyway, you do have such an awful voice for first thing in the morning. It sounds worse than a cats' choir."

"Waaark!" squawked Flewy. "Cats! Don't mention cats!" He shuddered at the thought. "After my last encounter with them, I still fly with a wobble and can't land properly. It really is most embarrassing."

Zag was about to switch off the radio when . . . "This is an urgent newsflash. Following the very severe lightning storms last night, news is coming in fast from around the world of mysterious happenings to famous landmarks and paintings. The Statue of Liberty has grown a beard, the Sydney Opera House roof has been flattened, the Eiffel Tower is bent double and the pyramids in Egypt are all now square-shaped. The lightning, always without thunder, struck . . ."

Flewy continued to grumble.

"Shush, I am trying to listen," said Zag, lifting his fez and scratching his head.

". . . More reports are coming in thick and fast from world-famous art galleries. Paintings, still hanging in their frames, have turned into a dark, sticky, porridgy mess . . ."

Flewy stared at Zag. "Okay, what's going on?"

"Don't look at me as if I have something to do with it."

"Who knows what side effects some of your thingummagadgetal inventions might cause?"

"Didn't you see the lightning last night?"

"What stupid lightning?"

"Surely you didn't manage to sleep through that?" said Zag, astonished.

"Sleep! That's what you're supposed do at night . . . unless of course you're a stupid owl," said Flewy irritably. "It strikes me the whole world is becoming stupid. The Statue of Liberty with a beard, square-shaped pyramids, smelly, messed-up paintings . . .Waaark, if you ask me, everyone's going completely nuts."

"Well, at least you escaped," said Zag.

"What from, the lightning?"

"No, the cats," said Zag, laughing.

"Waaark!" squawked Flewy. "Don't mention

CATS!"

Zag looked at his watch. "Is that the time already? Come on, we must fly."

"FLY as in aeroplane?"

"Yes, only this isn't, and it's much faster."

Zag left a very confused-looking Flewy and went into the barn. As he climbed the ladder to his bedsit loft to fetch his small suitcase, he pondered on the newsflash. He wished he could discuss it with someone, but it was pointless trying to have a meaningful conversation with Flewy, or even Awoo for that matter.

Zag returned to the Thingking Pad raring to go, wearing his bright blue Thingummajacket full of Thingummagadgets. He picked up the present he had neatly wrapped in brown paper.

"Much faster than an aeroplane?" squawked Flewy, still utterly baffled.

"Come along, shake a leg . . . or, in your case, a feather," chuckled Zag . "We are going to beamsurf."

"BEAMSURF!" exclaimed Flewy, suddenly worried about what he might be letting himself in for.

The Beamsurfer

Flewy's natural curiosity temporarily overcame his fear of the unknown as he followed Zag into the large, thatched barn. Strewn everywhere were all sorts of Thingummagadgets Immediately Flewy started fiddling and beaking around.

"Will you put that down!" said Zag. "You'll get all sticky."

Flewy was already in a right old mess. "What is this stuff, anyway?"

"It's dough-glue," said Zag, taking it out of harm's way.

Flewy tried preening himself without success. "I'm afraid it works a bit too well on feathers," he mumbled, with his beak stuck to his tail.

Zag fetched a damp cloth. "It's not meant for feathers. It's for sticking sliced bread back together." He wiped his fingers and handed the cloth to Flewy to sort himself out.

Some of Zag's Thingummagadgets were very daft: rubber scissors for cutting jelly; a friendly scarecrow that made birds happy; a computerized pudding that could save extra slices; a watch that went backwards to prevent you being late; and there were many more.

Some Thingummagadgets were so daft they were in fact very clever. The Beamsurfer was very special indeed. This particularly clever thingummagadgetal craft could "surf" along a selected beam of light. Using a mirrored satellite far in outer space, Zag could focus the special periscope mounted on top of the Beamsurfer and capture the reflected image of wherever he wanted to go. The energy absorbed from the beam propelled the craft at great speed.

Zag pulled open the huge wooden doors and proudly watched his friend's reaction.

Flewy was beak-smacked. He gazed upon the Beamsurfer in absolute amazement. It looked a little bit like a very sleek helicopter sitting upon two Frisbees, placed on top of a silver surfboard, and at the end of its long, thin tail was a shiny star. The unusual surface of the Beamsurfer gleamed in the shafts of sunlight that had found their way through the holes in the roof of the rickety barn.

"I developed the idea from the submarine periscope. It can take us anywhere in a flash," Zag said proudly, kicking some empty containers aside.

"So this is what you have spent so much time on," said Flewy. It certainly looked very impressive, but he had his doubts. "Are you really sure it will work?"

"Of course it works," said Zag confidently. "Get in and I will show you. We will arrive at Skagrock Bay in no time at all."

They had just settled inside the Beamsurfer when Zag jumped out of his seat. "Silly me, I have left my suitcase and the twins' birthday present outside," he said, clambering across the cockpit.

"Don't leave me alone in here. Something may happen," said Flewy, feeling very nervous indeed.

"Nothing will happen without me," said Zag, as he stepped on to the barn floor.

Suddenly the Beamsurfer came to life, as if it had a mind of its own. The door slammed shut and Flewy found himself trapped inside. Dials whizzed around, out of control, lights darted all over the cockpit and the large screen in front of him showed myriad flashing pictures. "Help! Help! HELP! Zag, where are you?"

"I am outside trying to get in, so stay where you are."

"I'm locked in, so how can I go anywhere?" squawked Flewy. "On second thoughts, maybe I am going somewhere. HELP !" he screeched.

"Let him take off on his own . . . and GOOD RIDDANCE," shouted Awoo from his lofty perch. Once again the owl had been woken up, but this time he was really enjoying the action below.

The Beamsurfer started shaking violently as Zag ignored Awoo and tried to wrestle the door open. "HAVE YOU ACCIDENTALLY LOCKED THE DOOR?" he shouted, making himself heard above the noise.

"WHICH DOOR?"

"THE ONLY DOOR," shouted Zag, fumbling around in his Thingummajacket. He hurriedly brought out a particular Thingummagadget, attached it to the door handle, pressed the green button and, with a big tug, opened the door.

Zag quickly threw his small suitcase into the cockpit and jumped in with the twins' present under his arm. Grabbing his chair, he sat down, flicked a switch and all became calm, with one noticeable exception. Flewy shook so much, his feathers seemed to be in danger of dropping off.

Zag screwed up his face. "I really must find out what causes this."

"Th. . .thanks a b. . .bundle. Th. . .that really is most reassuring," stammered Flewy. "That's it. I'm off."

But it was too late. Zag had already pressed more buttons. A deep swishing noise rapidly rose to a very high pitch, finally becoming barely audible. This time there was no shaking, just a soft sound similar to that of a distant hair-dryer. "Fasten your safety belt," he commanded.

Flewy was far too frightened to say anything and for once did exactly what he was told. He nervously watched Zag rotate a small joystick as an image of the Earth's surface appeared on the large screen.

"W. . .what is happening? Are we moving yet?" he asked.

Zag was busy pressing buttons, as numbers kept appearing and disappearing on a smaller screen. "I am just setting the co-ordinates to locate Skagrock Bay and lock the beam into the twins' cottage." He pressed another button, rotated the joystick once more, and up on the big screen came a picture of the twins' back garden.

"OOPS! We must avoid that," said Zag, making a few final minor adjustments.

"Avoid what?"

"William and Lucy's mum would go potty if we flattened her greenhouse." Zag double-checked his instruments. "That should be all right now," he said confidently.

"Only *should* be?"

"Everything will be all right." Zag smiled. "Now sit back and enjoy the trip."

He pulled a lever slowly back to halfway and the Beamsurfer gently lifted one metre off the ground, obediently rotating 180 degrees. With a terrific whoosh, it then took off through the big open barn doors and suddenly they were surfing the beam.

"H. . .how long will it take to get there?" asked Flewy.

"About five minutes. We are beamsurfing at nearly 2000 miles per hour." Zag sat back in his seat, turned away from the screen and looked at Flewy. "Well, it is automatic from here on in . . . that is, except for the 'tack' manoeuvre."

"What is a tack manoeuvre?" Flewy asked with some concern.

"When we need to change direction, we have to jump light beams because they only travel in straight lines," came the matter-of-fact reply. "It's sort of similar to sailing."

Flewy thought for a second. "Then how do we turn corners?"

A loud buzzer and a flashing red light took care of the answer. Zag immediately switched the Beamsurfer to manual control. Flewy broke out in a cold sweat, beads of perspiration rolling down his forehead and on to his yellow beak. Zag pulled at various levers with one hand while trying hard to control the joystick with the other. "You had better make sure your seat belt is securely fastened. This will be a very bumpy ride," he advised.

A big heavy jolt shook the craft so violently it nearly made Flewy swallow his stomach. Zag lost his grip on the joystick, the large monitor flashed snowy dots and the picture of the twins' garden vanished off the screen. The Beamsurfer bounced around worse than a speed boat racing in a heavy sea.

Flewy, having now discovered that Zag had not yet perfected a way of turning corners smoothly, was desperately trying to steady himself with his wings. "H. . .have w. . .we turned, I mean, t. . .tacked yet?"

Another heavy jolt made Zag's finger slip. "OOPS! Wrong button," he said.

The large monitor flickered back into life. This time it showed a very different destination, but the outline of the country was familiar.

"Fancy Australia?" Zag joked.

"Anywhere, just get me safely down on the ground," pleaded Flewy.

"Such a shame light doesn't curve naturally," said Zag, calmly pressing the co-ordinate memory button. He pointed to the large screen. "See, Flewy, no problem, there's Skagrock Bay." Zag moved the joystick a little to the right. "And there's the twins' garden." A green light flashed and he pressed a button to switch back to automatic. "Job done," he said with a broad smile. "Only two minutes to landing."

Flewy was not convinced. At that precise moment two minutes sounded longer than a lifetime.

The Arrival

The Beamsurfer landed gently in the garden and Zag busied himself shutting down the controls. Flewy was very quiet – just relieved that they had landed safely in the right spot.

As the whirring of the Beamsurfer died down, they heard the excited voices of the twins running towards the craft. Zag stepped out of the door on to the lawn, to be immediately beset by Lucy and William, asking a barrage of excited questions about the Beamsurfer.

"I will tell you all about it later," said Zag, hugging them tightly.

"Hi, Flewy," the twins shouted.

"Happy birthday." Flewy waved a wing and for once looked on patiently, with a big, beaky smile.

"Right, let me go now," said Zag. "We don't want to worry the neighbours, so the quicker I invisibilize the Beamsurfer, the better."

Lucy and William watched as Zag went back into the Beamsurfer and then re-emerged with his small suitcase and their all-important present.

"Can I do anything ?" asked Flewy, recovered from his ordeal.

"You can as a matter of fact." Zag fumbled around deep inside his Thingummajacket. "Here," he said, holding out his hand, "take the end of this for me."

Flewy could not see anything in Zag's hand. "Can you see anything?" he asked the twins, hoping the eventful journey had not driven him completely bonkers.

"Not a thing," said Lucy.

William inspected Zag's hand as closely as possible and shook his head. "Nor me."

"Well, that's a relief," sighed Flewy. "Come on, Zag, stop messing about."

"I'm not messing about. Now, please take this end in your beak and fly over the front of the Beamsurfer as I pull my end over the back."

Zag attempted to place the end in Flewy's beak, but Flewy kept moving his head and snapping at thin air. Lucy and William went into fits of laughter.

"Ouch! That was my finger. Would you mind keeping your head still . . . Please!" cried Zag.

"This is so stupid, it's making me go cross-eyed." But Flewy stayed still, felt something and grasped it firmly in his beak.

"At last," said Zag, sighing. "Okay, Flewy, now fly over the top and down on to the ground the other side."

The most amazing thing happened. The front of the Beamsurfer began to disappear, and as Zag clambered around the rear, so did the rest of the craft.

Zag gave a chuckle. "My Thingummagadgetal Invisibilizing Sheet . . . Good, isn't it?" he said with pride.

"Except for the fact that the star on the tail is still showing," observed Flewy, trying hard not to let on how impressed he really was.

"Drat it," said Zag.

"At least you managed to miss the greenhouse," said Flewy sarcastically, "although our journey took rather longer than you anticipated."

Zag beamed a tolerant broad smile. "Right," he said, looking at the twins, "which of you wants to carry this present?"

"I see that Lucy and William are about to be spoilt again," said the twins' mum, smiling as she watched them make their way down the steps to the patio of the old fisherman's cottage. "Be careful you don't trip over Mike's lobster pots," she warned. The twins' dad kept a very tidy ship, but such tidiness was confined to his trawler.

"Well, well, Sally-Anne, you look absolutely delightful," Zag said.

"You always say the sweetest things . . . you old charmer." She laughed and kissed him on the cheek. "Mike shouldn't be long. He left first thing to check for damage on the trawler after last night's storm."

"It's probably turned into a Jumbo Jet by now," said Flewy, butting in on the conversation in an attempt to get their attention.

"Anyway, I have to leave for London in half an hour or so," Sally-Anne continued. "The Tate Gallery has asked for my advice on how to restore the paintings."

"I thought you looked business-like today," said Zag.

"I imagined I would have a quiet life when I bought that small art gallery here in the town," she sighed.

"Obviously they need expert advice urgently," said Zag, grinning. "Mind you, it's all a bit strange, to say the least."

"In my opinion, the world's gone totally bonkers."

"Hi, Flewy, still making your presence felt!" Sally-Anne chuckled.

"How on earth can lightning affect paintings?" said Flewy. "I put it all down to people messing about with the bozo layer."

"Ozone layer. Bozo means idiot," said Zag.

Sally-Anne laughed as she put her arms around her twins. "Well, I won't be back until late tonight," she said, giving William and Lucy an extra squeeze, "but I promise I'll make it up to you later for missing out on your birthday and the midnight trawling expedition."

"Midnight trawling expedition!"exclaimed Flewy. "You know how easily I get   seasick!"

Zag smiled mischievously. "Fancy me forgetting to tell you about that."

The Thingummagadgetal
Birthday Present

They were all in the kitchen when Mike arrived, brandishing two long, thin parcels.

"It's Dad with some FISHING RODS," William shouted, to the deliberate annoyance of Lucy.

"How on earth did you know?" Mike pretended to be disappointed. "Ah, but I can see one that you won't guess," he said, nodding towards Zag's present.

"Let's open it in the lounge," said Sally-Anne, carrying a large pot of coffee and a plate of doughnuts out of the kitchen.

Once in the lounge, Zag carefully laid the large flat parcel on the floor.

William tore open the brown paper, revealing a slim, highly polished square carrying case. Lucy gently opened the lid to find a collapsible easel. Underneath sat a gold-coloured frame that held a taut artist's canvas, woven in a silvery, silk-like thread. The sunlight shining through the window made the framed canvas glimmer in a host of colours as she carefully lifted it from the case.

William delved further, discovering a pocket neatly set in the lid. Inside were two unusual-looking, silvery-handled painting brushes with fine glass-fibre bristles. The twins were completely fascinated. Zag's presents were always unusual, to say the least, and this one was no exception.

Sally-Anne was especially intrigued. "Maybe one day both of you will paint pictures that will hang in the Tate Gallery . . . Talking of which," she said, looking at the grandmother clock, "where's that taxi? I will miss the train."

Mike was about to offer to drive her to the station, when the taxi turned up. With her coat half on, she blew everyone a kiss.

Zag waved goodbye. "Good luck in resolving the mystery of the paintings."

Mike and the twins followed her to the doorstep. Sally-Anne gave them all a quick hug. "Love you lots. I'll probably be fast asleep by the time you return from your fishing trip."

Mike handed over her briefcase and, with a wink, shut the taxi door. The three of them waved as they watched the taxi bump its way down the cobbled hill and disappear around the corner.

Back in the lounge, Lucy and William once again became engrossed in their present.

"Well, I suppose it looks harmless enough, which is more than I can say about that Beamsurfer," muttered Flewy.

"So that's how you arrived here," said Mike. "You've been busy on that invention for months, Zag. It must be working well."

"That's a matter of opinion," said Flewy.

Zag ignored Flewy and carried on with the demonstration. "You don't even need paint. The brushes have their own very special thingummagadgetal power," he said with great pride. "I will show you how it all works."

"Cool," said William.

"Here we go again," muttered Flewy with an impatient sigh.

Zag quickly assembled the present. Pulling each leg of the easel out like a telescope, he stood it firmly on the floor, then positioned the framed canvas on it. "I will now demonstrate how you can paint as well as any artist, dead or living," he proudly announced. "Flewy, please take hold of this brush." Zag paused for thought, lifted his fez and scratched his forehead. "Okay, Flewy, place the brush anywhere on the canvas and think tree. Yes, that's it, let's keep it simple . . . think tree."

"Think tree! What do you mean, 'think tree'?" said Flewy, totally lost as to what he was being asked to do.

"Just imagine a tree," said Zag.

"What sort of tree?"

"Now don't be awkward," said Zag. "Think of any tree you like."

"Any tree?"

"Any tree," said Zag.

"OKAY, I'm thinking." A big, beaky, mischievous grin emerged on Flewy's face. The brush in his beak swiftly took control, forcing his head to go up, down, around and sideways as it painted a picture. The sight of all this nodding and twisting made the twins and their dad roar with laughter.

"What sort of tree is that" said Zag.

"A giant LAVATREE!" said Flewy, dropping the brush and rolling about on the floor in stitches.

Zag chuckled and picked up the second painting brush. Everybody was laughing so much they didn't notice it start to glow, first red, then yellow, then green. Zag drew an invisible circle on the floor.

"Attention please, everybody. For the next part of my demonstration I need all of you to stand next to me."

Still laughing, Mike, Lucy, William and Flewy

did what was asked of them. Zag touched the silvery canvas with the painting brush. The circle became visible, and they all disappeared into a fluorescent green, tubular whirlwind of light.

"W. . .where are we?" Flewy's voice echoed around the gleaming white, shiny cavern in which they found themselves.

Zag doubled up with laughter. "We're all inside your giant lavatory."

"This is not funny. Someone could come and flush us away," said Flewy, who was not fond of practical jokes that backfired on him.

"No fear of that," chuckled Zag. "We are only inside your painting."

"I must admit, to be stuck down a toilet, even if it's not real, has never been a great ambition of mine," laughed Mike.

"This would make a great ski slope," said Lucy, sliding around the bowl.

"Look out! I can see a big fat bottom," shouted William.

"Where? Where?" panicked Flewy.

"Just above the seat . . . it's okay . . . it's gone now." William continued to tease.

"Do you mind if we leave now?" said Flewy irritably.

Zag pointed the painting brush up at the white

toilet seat above them. "Just one last thing before we go back. Watch carefully and see what happens."

A brilliant ray of light sparkled out of the clear fibre bristles and the toilet seat turned each colour of the rainbow – red, orange, yellow, green, blue, indigo and finally violet.

"Cor, that's really cool," said Lucy.

"You see, even when inside the painting you can change anything to any colour you wish." Zag was proud as well as relieved that all was working well.

"Clever, but pointless," said Flewy. "Now, if you all don't mind, I wish to go back before my cup of coffee gets too cold."

"I can assure you that when we return, we will arrive back at the same time we left," said Zag.

Flewy looked at Mike and the twins. "I hope his time-keeping is not dependent on his Thingummagadgetal Watch that goes backwards."

Zag drew the invisible circle around them again and they all disappeared into the fluorescent green whirlwind of light.

They arrived back in the lounge in exactly the same spot and at exactly the same time as when they left. Even Flewy's coffee was exactly the same temperature as it had been at his last sip.

The Ghostly Galleon

Situated at the top of a steep and narrow cobbled lane, Fisherman's Cottage was little more than a stone's throw away from the small but busy fishing harbour where Mike moored his trawler.

"Better check the weather before we leave," he said, turning on the radio to hear the shipping forecast later that night.

They listened through the sea areas until finally the announcer said, ". . . and Skagrock, calm seas with good visibility . . ."

"Excellent," said Mike."

"Now for the latest news update. Earlier today the President of the United States talked at length over the hot-line with the Prime Minister. A global video-conferencing facility has been set up to allow various experts and heads of state to hold emergency talks regarding the mysterious things that have been happening to famous landmarks, paintings and other international works of art. We are still awaiting the official outcome of these discussions. However, we have been unofficially informed that scientists consider that the lightning storm has possibly triggered off some kind of unusual electrostatic reaction in the ozone layer, which might have affected the landmarks and paintings . . . "

"Hear that, Zag," said Flewy, looking very smug indeed. "Ozone, eh!"

Zag lifted his fez and scratched his head in disbelief. "Seems like they might have found an explanation."

"We are just receiving news that Big Ben has turned into a factory chimney and is billowing thick black smoke all over the Houses of Parliament. The beard on the Statue of Liberty has reached the ground and shows no signs of stopping. We will keep you up to date as we receive more news."

Mike turned the radio off. "Well, at least the weather is good. They don't forecast lightning and the sea will be like a millpond."

"Does anybody happen to have any seasickness pills?" asked Flewy meekly.

"Come on, let's go," said William, pulling at Lucy's arm. He didn't want to give Flewy a chance to spoil things at the last minute.

* * *

Zag loved visiting Skagrock Bay. He was in his element enjoying the fresh night sea-air as he walked down to the trawler, chatting about the Beamsurfer with Mike. To emphasize his points, Zag made sweeping gestures with his arms. They seemed an odd pair, especially with him being so short and Mike so tall. Added to which, Flewy reluctantly trailed behind, rudely mimicking Zag and hopping from one foot to the other.

Mike had taken a keen interest in Zag's inventions ever since Zag had used one of his Thingummagadgets to rescue him from certain death This had happened just before the twins were born. Mike survived to build a reputation for being the best trawler skipper around and, even better, a fantastic dad. Not surprisingly, as a result, Zag had always been treated as a very special member of the family.

As they turned the corner and the trawler came into view, William raced Lucy down to the quay-side.

"Go carefully on those cobbles," shouted Mike.

Bored with his own antics and the noticeable lack of attention they were getting him, Flewy took off after them.

Zag smiled. "Skagrock Bay is certainly the place to be," he said contentedly, taking a deep breath and looking at the full moon as they approached the boat.

"Welcome to my other Sally-Anne," said Mike proudly.

He had named the trawler after his wife, figuring that way she would always be with him. He introduced Zag and Flewy to the crew of five, who had been busily preparing the trawler.

"All shipshape and ready to go, Cap'n," said one of them.

"Thanks, Jim. I'll take her out of the harbour, then you can take over. We will fish about one and a half miles off Skagrock Point."

"Aye, aye, Cap'n," said Jim.

"Everybody, make sure your life-jackets are properly fastened before venturing out on deck," Mike instructed.

"Shall I find something for Flewy?" Lucy giggled.

"A sick bucket might be appropriate," said Zag, laughing.

"Oh, very funny," said Flewy, not amused and already feeling rather queasy.

The sturdy diesel engines rattled into life and they cast off. Mike carefully navigated his way out to the open sea and the crew busied themselves putting away the mooring warps.

Lucy and William watched the shore lights getting smaller and the trail of green and red lights flashing on their respective bobbing buoys.

Mike switched on the Tannoy. "Okay, Jim, you can take over now."

Jim entered the wheel-house. "It's a beautiful clear night out there, Cap'n, and the sea's as smooth as glass."

"I will stay here, if you don't mind," said Flewy, who had acquired a definite sickly green tinge to his feathers.

Mike smiled at Zag. "I won't try to convince him the fresh air will do him good."

It was all exactly as Jim had said. The clear dark sky allowed every star to twinkle its own secret message. Zag pointed out some of the formations with their names to Lucy and William. The full moon laid a shimmering golden carpet across the sea, as if offering an exclusive pathway to the mysteries of the heavens.

Mike sucked slowly at his empty pipe and checked his watch. "Nearly there. I think we can cast out the nets soon."

The engines started to fade a little as the trawler slowed down.

"Ready when you are, Cap'n," Jim called out.

Zag and the twins watched at a safe distance as the crew winched out the huge net. Unfolding itself, the net splashed into the sea.

"Fishing is better when the sea is rougher, but we will see what happens. This is normally a good spot," said Mike, taking the twins' fishing rods out of their canvas cases. "We will fish off the port bow so as not to risk the fishing lines snagging the nets when the boat circles."

The air was filled with the sound of the trawler's engines patiently chugging away, as Mike and Zag helped the twins cast their fishing lines.

"Sorry to interrupt, Cap'n," said Jim, rushing over to them, "but there's a weird, dense patch of swirling mist about thirty degrees off our starboard bow."

"How odd," remarked Mike, as the others followed him across the deck to take a look. "It's not the right weather conditions for a mist."

"It's odd, all right," said Flewy, as he fluttered up beside them, deciding there was safety in numbers. "That is the Ghost of the Black Galleon."

"Now is not the time for your nonsense," said Zag firmly.

"It's not nonsense. I have seen it once before, when I used to live around this coast," protested Flewy. "I don't mind admitting, I'm scared."

"Well, in all my many trips along this coast, I have never seen it before. It's just a fisherman's tale," said Mike.

Jim looked con-
cerned. "Sorry, Cap'n,
but I know other fisher-
men who have seen it.
They say it is sailed by a
cut-throat pirate called
Cap'n Terry Bull."

They watched in
awe as the black bow of
a huge galleon emerged
eerily from its dark,
swirling cloak into the
moonlight. Lucy and
William huddled close to their father. "We'll be all
right, I promise," he said. "Switch off the lights, Jim,
and keep us at a safe distance."

"Aye, aye, Cap'n," said Jim, rushing off to carry
out his orders.

"F. . .fisherman's tale, eh?" said Flewy,
shivering with fright.

"Has it been known to hurt anyone?" Zag asked
quietly.

"A. . .all I know is this Captain Bull used to
plunder ships and throw the crews overboard,"
whispered Flewy, trying to control his shaking.

The sinister black galleon slinked into full view
with the exception of its tall masts, the tops of which

were still partially hidden by the mist. The huge black sails appeared to bulge with the strain of the wind – but what was so very strange was that there was no wind.

Momentarily bound by fear and curiosity, Zag and the others didn't realize how close they were drifting towards this dark, fearsome ship.

"Look, I can see two of the crew moving about," said William.

Zag strained to see. "They would appear to be fighting!"

"One of them has thrown something overboard," said Lucy.

To their horror, the dreadful galleon changed tack, turning so that it was on a direct collision course with the *Sally-Anne*. "Whatever it is can stay in the sea," squawked Flewy. "Just take me home, please."

"Look after the twins," Mike shouted as he rushed to the wheel-house. He was very worried, knowing there was no time to cut loose the nets, which, left dragging in the sea, would slow down any manoeuvre he made.

The huge black bow of the galleon bore down on them, threatening to slice the *Sally-Anne* in two. Mike managed to turn the trawler, but not quite enough, and it hit the side of the galleon. An icy chill blew over the *Sally-Anne* as it miraculously passed right through the black hull, emerging on the other side without any damage whatsoever.

"How did you do that, Zag?" Flewy asked.

"I can't take any credit for it. We have just sailed through a ghost ship," Zag replied, watching the galleon sail on its way and wondering about its destination.

Mike had already begun to distance the *Sally-Anne* from the ghostly ship as it re-entered its swirling, black shroud and mysteriously disappeared into thin air, without leaving a trace of mist. He switched on the lights and his voice boomed over the Tannoy. "Jim, take over." Then he called out to the rest of the crew, "Haul in the nets, lads, and let's get out of here." Making straight for the twins, Mike held them tight and asked, "You two okay?"

The shock of what they had all witnessed meant that little was said as the crew winched in the nets. The catch was very small indeed, so it was totally unexpected when the winch motor suddenly began to strain a little.

"There is something fouling the net, Cap'n," shouted one of the crew. He looked over the side. "Whatever it is has wedged the net against the stern."

Mike helped the crew and after a short struggle they managed to free the net and pull the offending object on board.

"This is interesting," said Zag, as he and Mike inspected the old wooden sea-chest that had been caught in the net.

Using a torch, they could make out the carved initials ETT. The sea-chest was very securely locked, so they decided to leave further investigation to when they were safely ashore.

A Look Inside the Sea-chest

It was the early hours of the morning when the *Sally-Anne* finally nestled back on to her moorings. The rest of the harbour-side was quiet as the crew finished off closing down the trawler.

"Hold on, I'll give you a hand," said Jim, helping Zag and Mike put the sea-chest on to a fish-crate trolley. "Must say, Cap'n, I'm glad we've got the day off today."

"Me too," said Mike.

"Thanks for all your help, Jim." Zag smiled.

"My pleasure . . . anyways, g'night all."

Jim rejoined the rest of the crew, waiting to go home. They waved and went on their way, full of the night's events and discussing the prospect of recounting the scary sea-tale to the locals, later that day, in the quay-side inn.

Flewy seized the opportunity of an effortless ride, as the twins, Mike and Zag pushed the sea-chest up the cobbled lane to Fisherman's Cottage. With much pushing and shoving, they finally wheeled the heavy load around the back of the cottage.

Flapping about on top of the sea-chest, Flewy tried to keep his balance as the others manoeuvred it through the kitchen door. "Left a little . . . no, I mean right a little . . . uh . . . no, left a little . . . uh, right . . . no, left . . ."

"It would be helpful if you knew right from left," said William, struggling with Zag at one end of the sea-chest.

"It would be even more helpful if you got off it," said Lucy, trying to open the door further than it was meant to go.

"Only trying to assist . . . that's all," said Flewy indignantly, as he fluttered into the kitchen.

"We must be quiet. Remember, Mum is fast asleep," whispered Mike, finally easing the chest through the door.

Watched intently by the others, Zag put on his half-rimmed glasses and set about the challenge of opening the sea-chest. He lifted his fez, scratched his head, then fumbled around inside his Thingummajacket, bringing out a bowl of red jelly that was covered in cling film.

"I thought we were trying to open the lock, not throw a party," said Flewy sarcastically.

"I know how you could be helpful," said Mike.

"How's that?"

"By shutting up for a minute," said Mike, sounding exasperated.

The twins chuckled as Flewy did his infamous seagull sulk, slapping his foot on the floor, wings on waist, and sticking his beak in the air.

"This happens to be my Thingummagadgetal Plopmould," said Zag patiently, scooping a handful out of the bowl. As he rolled it into a sausage shape, it took on a Plasticine-like texture. With some difficulty, he started to push and ease the floppy substance into the lock.

"You would have more chance inserting a marshmallow into a slot machine." Flewy could not keep his beak shut.

Zag peered over his glasses. "If I can get sufficient inside this lock quickly enough, my irritating friend, it will form itself into the correct shape, set like steel and become a key." He gave another push and tuck, and the Plopmould plopped into place and hardened within seconds. "That should do it." With one easy turn, the lock snapped open. "See, it does work," said Zag with a broad grin.

"Well done," said Lucy.

"What's inside?" William asked, unable to stand the suspense any longer.

"Shush, keep the noise down!" said Lucy.

Zag lifted the hinged lid and looked inside.

"Well?" said Flewy pompously. "I hope all our efforts have been worth it."

The inside of the sea-chest was completely waterproof and had an upper compartment. Zag found a silvery metal orb, about twice the size of a tennis ball, fitted snugly into a black velvet-lined tray. He carefully lifted it out. "I have never seen metal quite like this before," he said, studying the orb closely.

"Looks more like mirrored glass to me," said William.

"It's definitely a metal of some sort . . . and look! Here's an inscription." Zag, even with his glasses on, couldn't quite make it out. "See if you can read it, Mike," he said, passing it to him.

Mike just made it out. "Protect within each fiery stone locked as one, each never alone." He looked puzzled. "What on earth does that mean?" Mike turned the orb around to see if there were any clues and found a stretched figure of eight etched into the metal. "Look, that's the sign of infinity," he said, passing it back to Zag.

Zag ran a finger over the etching. To everyone's surprise, the top half of the orb clicked open, nearly spilling its contents. With a juggle, he just managed to save a misty, greyish stone from falling on the floor. It was shaped like a quarter segment of an orange with a stubby, key-like prong protruding from one flat side. On the opposite side was a small keyhole of the same diameter.

"This stone is one quarter of a perfect sphere," said Zag, examining it closely. "I wonder what happened to the other three stones?"

"Maybe there's something else in the sea-chest that could give us a clue as to what this is all about," suggested Lucy.

Zag pulled out the tray to check if there was anything else underneath. The base of the sea-chest was loose; he gently pressed it and a lid sprang open. "What have we here?" he said, lifting out an extremely dark, murky painting and putting it on the kitchen table to give everyone a better view.

"It's a tropical island, painted in dull, horrible colours," said Lucy.

"I wouldn't fancy going there on holiday," remarked William.

"Probably infested with cats," said Flewy, with a shiver.

Zag lifted up his fez. "I am sure I recognize this from somewhere. I might have seen it in an old book or something," he said, scratching his head.

"It's so gloomy it would be difficult to forget," Mike commented.

Zag looked for the artist's signature. All he could find was a dirty smudge at the bottom right-hand corner. "Looks odd to me, but then I'm not an expert like Sally-Anne."

"Well, the expert is fast asleep," said Mike, noticing Lucy and William yawning. "I think we will ask her opinion over breakfast, with fresh minds. Meanwhile, it's well past bedtime."

Zag carefully placed the orb back in the sea-chest. "Good idea," he said, wishing for some quiet in which to think over everything.

"Sally-Anne has prepared the guest bedroom," said Mike.

"Yes, thank you very much," said Zag.

"And puffed up the old doggy bean-bag for Flewy," said Lucy, chuckling.

"What! The one that next-door borrowed for their tom-cat?" teased William.

"Thank you kindly, I'm sure," said Flewy, not at all amused.

Mike gave a big yawn. "Come on, you two, say good-night," he said, as he ushered the children up the stairs with him.

"Flewy and I won't be long either," Zag called up quickly after them. "Sleep well."

He picked up the painting and took it into the lounge. He carefully placed it on the easel and stood back, looking at it thoughtfully.

Flewy dozed, and for a short while nothing was said, until the silence was broken by loud snores resounding from Mike and Sally-Anne's bedroom.

"Great!" said Flewy, waking up. "Can't even doze, let alone sleep with that racket."

As if on cue, two pairs of feet crept down the stairs, went into the lounge and stood beside Zag, in front of the painting.

Zag peered sternly over his half-rimmed glasses

at the twins, who were still fully dressed. "You'll get me into trouble if your dad wakes up and finds you back down here."

Flewy, irritated by being woken up and noticing the twins' painting brush nearby, could not resist fiddling with it. He started waving it around and around, inadvertently drawing a circle. The brush started to glow red, then yellow, then green. Too late, Zag realized what was happening. He grabbed the brush from Flewy, but he accidentally touched the canvas with it.

In a split second the fluorescent green whirlwind of light whisked the four of them into the horrors of the murky painting.

The Stranger in the Dark, Tropical Woods

They found themselves in a clearing situated in the middle of a dense, tropical wood. Above them loomed a thick, dark cloud that covered the tall palm trees like an undertaker's blanket. Day or night could pass and never be noticed. All was deathly quiet, except for the occasional nervous flapping of Flewy's wings.

"Was that you, Flewy, or did I hear something?" said Zag.

They all huddled together and listened hard, but could hear nothing.

"I'm f. . .frightened enough already without you joking around," complained Flewy.

"Serves you right for getting us into this mess," Lucy scolded.

"Take us home, Zag," pleaded Flewy. "I'll be good, honest."

"I wish I could, my friend, but. . ."

A breeze disturbed the still air and immediately developed into a gale-force wind. Something roared as it flew past like a tornado, close above the trees. Out of the dark clouds, blinding white lights flashed in all directions. Flewy was knocked over and carried a short distance by the turbulence that followed. Then all was quiet once more.

"Help, where are you?" Flewy cried out from the darkness.

"We are over here," said Zag. "We're looking for the painting brush. It fell out of my hand as we landed."

"We had two brushes," said William.

"The other is back at Fisherman's Cottage," said Zag.

"Oh, great! That's all we need," Flewy moaned.

"There's no time to argue. We must find it," said Zag, searching through the thick undergrowth. "With luck, it should be close by."

"Okay, then, I'll help . . . I'm scared, that's all," said Flewy indignantly, hoping he didn't come across any creepy-crawlies.

"We're all scared, but we must keep ourselves under control to have any chance of getting out of here," said Zag.

Without warning, another breeze disturbed the still air, quickly developing into a strong, gusting wind. This time Flewy was prepared. He held on firmly to Zag.

Blinding lights flashed and the wind roared as a large sinister craft flew at high speed close above the trees. Zag managed to look up during the turbulence and saw a sliver of blue sunlit sky as the dark blanket of cloud was torn apart ever so slightly. The sinister craft powered towards the distant shaft of sunlight to join another craft, leaving the turbulence to quickly fade away in its wake.

"Look! They're chasing something," shouted William.

Zag reached deep inside his Thingummajacket and pulled out his Vistascopic Bubblegum, popped it in his mouth, briefly chewed at it, wished it tasted less like postage stamps and blew a large, clear bubble. He held the bubble in the air and the flying images could be clearly seen as if on a television screen. "Chasing two things more like," he said, studying it closely.

Before he could make out exactly what was happening, another series of blinding flashes seared across the sky and the thick cloud sealed away the rays of sunlight, leaving them in total darkness once again.

A piercing POP! made Flewy all but jump out of his feathers. "W. . .what's that? What's th. . .that? W. . .what's thaaaaaat?" he screeched, ducking for cover under Zag's Thingummajacket.

"Me popping my Vista-bubble." Zag chuckled.

Flewy cautiously beak-peeped out between the tail vents of Zag's Thingummajacket. "Y. . .you half s. . .scared me to death."

Lucy giggled at this absurd sight. "Don't be silly, it wasn't that loud."

"Don't care how loud it was," said Flewy huffily, emerging from his somewhat unusual hideaway. "I want to get out of here."

"Then help us," said Zag, free from the rather personal intrusion and resuming the search with Lucy and William to find the painting brush.

"It's all your fault we're here in the first place," chipped in William.

"That's it . . . blame me . . . blame me," Flewy flapped.

"Anyway, who invented your stupid present, then, eh?"

"Shush! Listen!" said Zag.

Flewy became super-glued with fear. His next remark had been completely overtaken by the distinct sound of the snapping of twigs.

From out of the dense trees a large shadowy creature appeared and rustled slowly towards them through the undergrowth. William picked up a stout stick, ready to strike out at the unknown danger.

Zag hurriedly fumbled deep inside his Thingummajacket and pulled out a Frisberang. A cross between a Frisbee and Boomerang, it had a central spindle that contained many yards of thread as fine as a spider's web, but as strong as the heaviest rope. It could be thrown accurately for a great distance and would return. Invented for lifeboats to attach to ships in trouble in heavy seas, Zag had never dreamed of needing to use it under these circumstances. He crouched low and prepared to launch the Frisberang at the creature, hoping the line would entangle it.

The creature came a little closer to them, then stopped for a moment. Two large, piercing yellow eyes stared silently at them from out of the gloom.

Zag cautiously ventured towards the shadowy creature. To his surprise, he discovered a rather large and forlorn-looking eagle. Flewy fluttered in fright at the sight of this monstrous bird.

In its menacing, curved beak the eagle held the broken painting brush. Placing the two pieces on the ground, it said softly, "I guess ya all are looking for these."

Zag picked up the valuable halves of the painting brush and thanked the eagle. Inspecting the damage as best he could in the darkness, he sighed. "At least it's not beyond repair, but it may take a little while to fix."

"See ya 'round . . . well, barely, under this sky," said the eagle miserably. "Take my advice, don't hang around here and don't walk too far over that way." He pointed with his very large wing. "If ya do, ya'll fall off the edge of the high cliff," he warned, "cos ya won't see it till it's too late."

No sooner had he spoken than the breeze began to rustle through the trees and quickly developed into a gale-force wind. Bright lights flashed and a large sinister craft flew past just above the trees.

"They're trying very hard to find us," the eagle said, ducking for cover.

"US? US?" squawked Flewy. "You, more like."

The eagle turned an exasperated expression on Flewy. "Believe me, pal, it's US!" he said.

"Who are they, and why are they searching for us?" William asked.

"I haven't a clue how ya all got here, but what I do know is ya have a lot to learn."

"Could you be kind enough to tell us what we need to learn?" Zag asked politely.

"Sure, but not now, cos we've really gotta hurry. They're bound to get us if we stay here," the eagle said, in a matter-of-fact sort of way. "Come on, ya'd better all follow me. Stay close behind."

"You walk well for an eagle," Lucy said.

"Plenty of practice," came the gloomy reply.

The Eagle's Cave

The journey seemed never-ending, made all the longer by having to tread cautiously through the murkiness of the dense, tropical woods.

Eventually they came to a clearing at the top of a craggy hill. From the distance came the sound of roaring wind. Looking back, they could see bright lights flashing and darting about in the sky above the spot where they had first met the eagle.

"They definitely would have got us all by now," said the eagle soberly.

"Who?" said Zag. "You must tell us what is going on."

"Why has this happened to me?" muttered Flewy despairingly.

"You mean US," said Lucy angrily, "don't you, Flewy?"

"We've got no time for arguments," said the eagle, urging them to move quickly. "We must make haste. Follow me."

"But I'm tired and fed up," Flewy protested.

"No time to be tired. Come on! Come on!" said the eagle impatiently, "or all will be lost." Ignoring Flewy, he turned to the others. "Doesn't that creature ever stop complaining?"

"You're getting to know him already," said Zag with a grin.

As they approached a cliff edge, they began to hear the torrential rush of water. The eagle stopped. "Now, ya guys, this final part is the most dangerous. We have to make our way around a narrow ledge. It's wet and very slippery, so be careful!"

The sound of rushing water became louder as they cautiously shuffled along the narrow pathway that precariously wound its way around the side of the cliff. It led them behind the huge waterfall that was now cascading in front of them.

"This is where I live," the eagle said.

"All the mod cons, I see . . .built-in high impulse shower and all that," quipped Flewy.

They followed the eagle ever so carefully along the slippery ledge into the gaping mouth of his huge cave. It was very dark inside and had a dreadful smell of damp, mouldy feathers and sweaty, horrible, droppy-type things that are far too unpleasant to describe.

Zag hastily reached into his coat, fumbled

around and pulled out a crystal and placed it on the floor. It started to glow and sizzle like sausages frying in a pan. It even smelt like sausages.

"My Thingummagadgetal Smellypong Remover," he gleefully explained, "with a built-in light of course," he added proudly.

"Yuk, greasy sizzling sausages," commented Flewy. "Still, at least it's better than the dreadful stink that was here before."

"We can see much better now," said Lucy quickly, hoping the eagle would not be offended by Flewy's indelicate remark.

Flewy spotted a large pile of twigs. "Look, we can build a fire."

"That's my bed, if ya don't mind," said the eagle gruffly. "Anyway, what a stupid suggestion. A fire would smoke us out."

"It's stupid for an eagle to live in a cave," argued Flewy.

"It's not out of choice, ya idiot. Anyway, I bet ya live in a tree."

"He does," said William.

"A seagull living in a tree. That's funny," said the eagle.

Flewy was not amused. Wings on hips, he pointed his beak in the air and slapped the ground repeatedly with one webbed foot.

"Come on, Flewy, where is your sense of humour?" asked Lucy.

"The exact same place as my sense of adventure," snapped Flewy.

Zag fumbled in his Thingummajacket and found his Thingummagadgetal Heavy-duty Micro-folding Thermal Ground Sheet, which he unfolded and laid on the floor of the cave. "Let's all sit down and decide what to do about this situation," he said, inviting the eagle to join him. "Now, first of all, how about telling us exactly where we are?"

"And who is searching for us?" said William.

"And why?" said Lucy.

"Yeah, in short, what's this horrible place all about?" said Flewy impatiently, slapping his foot on the ground again.

"Will ya stop banging ya foot, ya annoying little bird?" said the eagle, staring at him angrily.

"Mutant parrot!" Flewy mumbled back under his breath.

The eagle sighed and stretched, spread his large wings, knocked Flewy sideways in the process, and then said, "Now, where shall I begin?"

Blot!

The unspoken consensus was that Flewy had received only a light reprimand from the eagle which could easily have been much worse. Zag would not have allowed it to go further and indeed was grateful to see the mischievous satisfaction in the eagle's eyes. The only thing that had been harmed was Flewy's ego, although from the fuss he made you might be forgiven for thinking he was damaged beyond repair.

"Welcome to the Island of Blot," said the eagle.

"Island of Blot!" exclaimed Lucy.

"Island of Splat, more like," laughed William, watching Flewy try in vain to gain sympathy with dramatic brushing-himself-down gestures.

"Yup, in the Kingdom of Erasure," the eagle replied.

"Where in the world is that?" asked Zag.

"Ya are in the darkest corner of the World of Creativity, which, to be precise, is in the Galaxy of Ideas."

"Well, how stupid of me. I should have guessed," mocked Flewy.

"So who is looking for us?" Zag quickly asked.

"Eraser the Terrible, the ruler of Blot. It is he who keeps the island in darkness," replied the eagle.

"Why is he doing that?" asked William.

"Cos he's evil and jealous of everything that's creative and beautiful, wherever it may be. He's determined to destroy it all," replied the eagle.

Zag lifted his fez and scratched his head. "So Eraser is trying to destroy not only the World of Creativity, but any world of his choosing?"

"Yup, he wants to rub it all out, then impose his nasty, grotesque ideas on . . . " The eagle stopped and assumed a very solemn expression before continuing, ". . . everywhere and everything."

"Including US?" Flewy asked.

"At last ya got it. YUP, including ya and me, pal, and that means US!"

"That does it! That really does it!" squawked Flewy.

"Just be quiet, Flewy," said Lucy.

"Those noises, the rush of wind and flashing lights, come from the Cameracraft, flown by his Eradicators. They hover, glide and swoop far better than any eagle. There's no escape, if they capture ya into their light."

"Amazing!" said Zag, engrossed. "A sort of flying camera which takes a photograph that captures all of you and not just your image."

"That's what happened to my mate." The eagle began to sob.

Deep in thought, Zag said, "Mmm, this is all very interesting."

"Interesting! Interesting!" squawked Flewy. "I'll tell you what's interesting: how long it will take for the painting brush to be fixed and for us to get out of here. Now that's what I call interesting!"

"Be patient," said Lucy.

"I'm trying, I'm trying," Flewy squawked. "But not only do we now have more complications, not only do we not have a clue what Mr Flipping Eagle is on about, we also have a . . . Come on now, be fair, who ever heard of a crying flipping eagle?"

"My name is not Mr Flipping Eagle."

"What is it then?" Flewy asked.

"Eggbert."

Flewy could not contain himself. "I'm gonna laugh, I'm gonna laugh, I'm . . . gonna . . . laugh. Eggbert the eagle, hahahahahaha, ooooeeeee, hehehe-hehehe, Eggbert . . . the . . . flipping . . . eagle," he spluttered, nearly choking .

Eggbert angrily spread his huge wings to chase

Flewy. "Hey, BUDDY, I'm having you for my supper."

"Nobody is eating anybody," said Zag, stopping Eggbert in his tracks.

Lucy quickly grabbed hold of Flewy. "He'll probably taste no better than his behaviour," she cried protectively.

"Yes, Eggbert, we'll help you and you can help us," William added.

"And this seagull is going to promise to behave," said Lucy, hoping the eagle would reconsider his threat. "Aren't you?" she prompted.

"I promise, I promise," said Flewy, fearing he was culinary history in the making.

"Well, that settles that," said Zag, finally cooling the situation. "Now, Eggbert, please tell us what happened to your mate."

Eggbert relented and continued his story. "We noticed that when the Cameracraft flew through the thick, black cloud, it left a hole that allowed in the sunlight. My mate, Eggna, tried to make for the hole, but it closed up too quickly. Another Cameracraft chased her, shooting its light, and the flash captured her."

The commotion Zag had seen in his Vistascopic Bubblegum now made sense. "Not long before you bumped into us?"

"Yup, that's right," said Eggbert sorrowfully.

"How did ya guess?"

"We saw it all happen," said William.

"Well, some of it," said Zag. "Why didn't you both hide in the dark cloud?"

"Too thick and sticky," replied Eggbert.

"Sounds like a sort of black porridge," said William.

"So where is your mate now?" asked Lucy

"Collage, most probably," Eggbert replied sadly.

"Collage?" asked Zag. "Is that another island?"

"No, a prison. A terrible, overcrowded, confusing place. Ya are stuck underneath and on top of all sorts of strangers and odd things. Once there, ya never ever leave. Ya true meaning is lost for ever."

"Just like one of those sweaty Spanish beaches," quipped Flewy.

"Ya wouldn't joke if Artless the Heartless caught ya."

"What do you mean by losing your true meaning?" asked William.

"This tropical island is no longer what it was originally created to be, so now it has lost its true meaning," explained Eggbert.

Zag was fascinated. "So your true meaning is your reason for being created in the first place. Lose your true meaning and you're lost for ever."

"Ya got it, Buddy. Hit the nail right on."

"Who is Artless the Heartless?" asked Zag.

"Collage is controlled by him. He's second-in command to Eraser."

"I'll sum it all up for you," said Flewy, desperate to leave as soon as possible. "We're stuck on the Island of Splodge. . ."

" BLOT," corrected Lucy.

"Whatever . . . BLOT, a one-time tropical island now completely covered in a dark cloud of porridge, in the Kingdom of Erasure, in the World of Creativity, which is in the Galaxy of Ideas, trying to escape from flying cameras, in a cave smelling of sausages, with an eagle called Eggbert, whose mate, Eggna, lost her being on a crowded beach that is controlled by a nasty piece of work called Artless the Heartless, an Eradicator, who happens to be the best friend of someone even nastier, called Eraser the Terrible."

Everybody applauded.

"Very good!" said William. "That is, except for the beach bit."

"The only thing that's good is the number of reasons there are to get out of here," said Flewy.

Suddenly a strong wind blew violently into the mouth of the cave, bringing a wave of water that caught everybody by surprise.

Flewy and Eggbert only just managed to fly on to a ledge out of harm's way. Zag succeeded in grabbing hold of William and clinging to a rock. But Lucy, caught up in the backwash of the subsiding water, was sucked towards the mouth of the cave and the raging waterfall beyond. Just in time, Eggbert swooped down, snatched her up in his talons and laid her gently down beside Zag.

"We owe you our gratitude. Thanks, Eggbert," said Zag.

"What are buddies for anyway?" said Eggbert, a touch embarrassed.

"Th. . .thanks, Eggbert," spluttered Lucy.

"That's okay, little lady, I needed the wash."

For a brief moment a stream of sunlight lit the corner of the entrance to the cave, but then it disappeared as the hole in the cloud sealed itself and the darkness returned.

"It is high time we did something to sort Eraser out," said Zag.

Dead Reckoning

Untroubled by the deep swell, the *Sea Err* lay in wait two miles off the coast of Blot. Except for the mizzen, the tall skeletal masts of the sinister galleon hung bare. The black, shroud-like sails furled against their spars, as if attempting to smother them.

Every time Eraser the Terrible went off on one of his rampages throughout the galaxy and elsewhere, he would separate the Orb of Brilliance and hide the four Stones. He had figured this way it would be harder for anyone to steal it from him. However, this return passage to Collage, a little further around the peninsula, had been totally disrupted. Before Eraser could think of how to recover his sea-chest, two eagles had swooped on deck and somehow stolen two more Stones.

Below deck at the stern of the ship, Eraser's rake-like figure paced up and down his cabin while he and Artless the Heartless waited for the two

Cameracraft to return with the captured eagles.

"I have lost . . . No . . . No . . . NOT ME! . . . You . . . yes, that's it, YOU!" Eraser raved. "YOU HAVE LOST ME the ORB and THREE of the STONES!"

"Surely separating them gave more chance for them to be stolen," said Artless.

"DON'T LECTURE ME! I'M IN COMMAND, NOT YOU!" Eraser's thin lips twitched angrily. "ACTUALLY there was less chance of them being completely stolen, AND THAT'S WHAT'S HAPPENED!"

Eraser's cabin was full of plundered antique furniture and fine art, all of which he loved to hate. He adjusted the splendid mirror, peered into it and, with spindly, bony fingers, squeezed the life out of an erupting boil situated on the tip of his hooked nose. "I put the Orb and the Stone of Skill in my sea-chest, hid the Stones of Imagination and Inspiration in my cabin, AND if it wasn't for the fact that I WEAR the Stone of Genius around my neck, THAT WOULD BE MISSING AS WELL!" Eraser stood back from the mirror, preened the ruffles of his orange silk shirt and adjusted the high lapels of his long purple coat. His thoroughly tasteless pirate finery clashed horribly with his pimply, pallid complexion. "AND how you managed to LOSE my sea-chest overboard BEATS

ME!"

"He's a very big Eradicator," said Artless, gesturing like an angler who had caught one "that size". "It went over as I struggled with him. And anyway, I didn't know that he'd previously placed the Stones of Imagination and Inspiration on the deck in readiness for those two eagles to swoop down and pick up. Would you like me to pour you a glass of wine?"

"Wine! WINE!" Eraser's sunken, bag-ridden, pig-like eyes positively bulged with fury under his unruly mane of long, frizzy ginger hair. "NO! NO! I want that traitor CAUGHT AND PUNISHED! I want those thieving Eagles CAUGHT AND PUNISHED!"

"I have the traitor Eradicator captive here on the ship," said Artless. "How would you like him to be pun . . ."

There was a knock on the cabin door. "The Cameracraft are coming into land, SAR," a crew member called out.

"And about time too!" said Eraser gruffly. He and Artless made their way on to the poop-deck to watch two eerie stingray-like shapes conduct their vertical landings.

A large telescopic lens formed the nose of the Cameracraft. Inset into their prow, a broad silvery diamond-shaped window held a powerful flashlight.

The two Cameracraft stealthily nestled down, taking their place in an orderly row alongside four others. Apart from the long flight deck positioned on its port side, the *Sea Err* camouflaged a host of secrets, making this sinister ship much more than a combination of galleon and Cameracraft carrier.

Two canopies hissed open, each releasing a helmeted, high-booted figure dressed in swashbuckling black. Their uniforms, strangely at odds with the sleek craft, ruffled in the wind as they swiftly made their way to the poop-deck. Removing their helmets, the two Eradicators stood smartly to attention in front of Eraser and Artless.

"IDIOTS! What took you so long?" said Eraser, angrily scuffling his fancy boots on the deck.

"We successfully managed to capture one eagle, Sar!" said an Eradicator nervously.

"We kept searching for the other, Sar!" added the second.

"AND!" Eraser bawled.

"We lost it, Sar!" replied the first.

Eraser shook his head and glanced at Artless. "That's all right then . . . they lost it." The full venom of his anger was mounting by the minute. "YOU LOST IT?"

"Yes, Sar! And we're sorry, Sar!" the other said

meekly.

"Truly sorry, Sar!" added the first.

Eraser spoke softly. "Sorry? So you're truly sorry?" He peered at Artless. "Hear that?" He turned his back on them and gazed up at the mizzenmast.

"I heard it," Artless nodded in reply.

"They're truly sorry . . . so that must be okay then." Eraser suddenly spun around to face the Eradicators. "I'LL SHOW YOU JUST WHAT TRULY SORRY MEANS!"

"Give me the image of the eagle," commanded Artless, stepping forward and ripping off the insignia of winged skull and wishbones from their lapels.

The first Eradicator delved nervously into his pocket and pulled out a "prismatran" the size of a playing card. It would have been transparent, except it now imprisoned Eggna. Her shocked holographic image looked as if it had been instantly frozen in clear ice.

Eraser snatched it out of the Eradicator's hand. "I want to see that first!" he growled. A sickly smile spewed over his scrawny face as he gazed evilly at the horrified eagle's image trapped inside and saw the Stone of Imagination. "Well, well, well, look what it is clutching in one of its talons."

Artless looked over Eraser's narrow shoulder. "Well, at least we have part of a result."

"You're the only one I can trust with this," said Eraser. "When we get to Collage, we'll extract the Stone from the eagle's image." He handed the prismatran to Artless and added threateningly, "Until then, you'd better make sure you put this somewhere very secure."

"Meanwhile, what do you want done with these two?" asked Artless.

"Ah yes, these idiots." Eraser seemed to lighten up. "Well, as their escapade was not entirely fruitless. . ."

"Oh, thank you, Sar!" interrupted one.

"Don't get too excited," Eraser scolded softly.

"AND DON'T INTERRUPT!" he bawled.

The Eradicators stood nervously to attention while Eraser took his time thinking, pacing up and down the short deck. Pausing in front of the Eradicators at last, he said, "I've decided I won't put you in Collage."

"Thank you, Sar!" said one.

"Very grateful to you, Sar!" said the other.

"I'm going to let you . . ." Enjoying the sight of the two Eradicators nearly dying with suspense, he suddenly broke into a fit of silly giggles . . . "WALK THE PLANK!" His manic laughter stopped abruptly. "ARTLESS, deal with these two imbeciles."

Eraser started to make his way down the steps to the quarter-deck, then called back, "And while you're at it, do the same to that TRAITOR who dared to try to steal my sea-chest, then meet me back in my quarters."

Eraser poured himself a goblet of fine wine, took a sip and opened his cabin window. Raising his goblet again, he counted three yells and splashes as Artless swiftly carried out his orders. Soon after, there was a knock on his cabin door.

"If you're not Artless the Heartless, PUSH OFF!"

Artless opened the door and poked his head

around. "You did say only three?"

Eraser scowled impatiently into his wine. "Come in and close the door!"

Artless looked around for his goblet of wine, but as usual none had been poured for him. "Just checking, that's all."

"I'd advise you to take matters more seriously from now on."

"Granted, things could be better."

"BETTER?" Eraser glared at Artless. "I didn't risk stealing the Orb of Brilliance from the Master of the Galaxy to have IT and THREE of the Stones stolen off me!"

"You still have the most powerful stone around your neck, we've recaptured the one with the eagle and we know that the other eagle has still got one," said Artless calmly.

"I KNOW THAT!" Spittle exploded out of Eraser's mouth with the fury of a high-pressured, frayed hose. "BUT your men either can't be trusted or have lost their touch. And if I didn't know better, maybe you . . ."

"Can't be trusted or have lost my touch?" Artless calmly interrupted.

"YOU TELL ME!" Eraser raged, plonking himself down behind his antique desk and glowering at Artless. "If we don't get our act together VERY

SOON, everything that exists, INCLUDING US, will turn into a thick gooey mess." He took an angry gulp of wine, forgot to swallow and sprayed, "WE'LL ALL BE PORRIDGE!"

"We've always sorted things before," said Artless. "Be patient."

"PATIENT?" Eraser banged his fist on the desk. "ARE YOU GOING NUTS?" His goblet bounced up in the air, spilling dark red wine over his clothes. "Now look what's happened!" he shouted, jumping up from his seat. "My clothes ruined, all because you can't do your job properly. WELL! ...DO SOME-THING!"

Artless picked up a few loose pages from the desk and started dabbing at the wet patches of wine.

"NOT THAT!" yelled Eraser, pushing him away. "Capture that other eagle AND RECOVER THE ORB AND MISSING STONES!"

No Time to Lose

Apart from being soaking wet, like the others, Lucy had recovered from her ordeal. The only thing to have been completely washed away was Eggbert's bed. The light from Zag's crystal, jammed by the force of the water between two large boulders, was now partially hidden.

"Well, at least the place has been cleaned," said Flewy, shaking his feathers.

"Pity we can't dry it out," said Eggbert.

"We need to dry ourselves out," said William, shivering.

"My Thingummagadgetal Bragbag should do the trick," said Zag, fumbling deep inside his Thingummajacket and pulling it out. "It is full of hot air, collected from all those people who boast about themselves," he said proudly.

"Hope it doesn't smell of bad breath," said Flewy.

Zag placed the Bragbag on the floor. "I must admit this particular invention was a challenge, and I was never sure what it would be useful for, until now," he said, untying the string from around the top.

The cave was suddenly filled with not only hot air but also all the noisy, bragging voices. "Mine's much bigger than that!" "I've got a better one than you!" "I am so handsome." "I am the best footballer in my school." "All the boys always want to kiss me." "I am so very clever . . . " The Bragbag went on and on and on.

"WHAT A RACKET!" shouted Eggbert, trying to make himself heard.

"Could you please TURN IT OFF!" yelled Flewy.

Zag fumbled in his Thingummajacket and pulled out some cotton wool. "Pity I didn't invent this stuff. It is really useful," he said to himself, as he put a piece in each ear and tied up the string on the Bragbag.

It wasn't until the noise stopped that the others noticed something had happened.

"That thing's wicked. It's nice and cosy in here now," said William.

"All our clothes are dry," said Lucy. "Oh, Zag, you are so clever." She kissed him on the cheek and asked, "Will the Bragbag collect that boast?"

"Pardon?" said Zag. "What did you say?" he

pulled the cotton wool from out of his ears.

"Will the Bragbag collect the boast I just made about you?" asked Lucy for the second time.

"No," he chuckled. "Because you complimented me. It will only collect a boast if someone brags about themselves."

"Why?" asked William.

"Because that is the only time when brags are full of hot air," laughed Zag.

William found the Heavy-duty Micro-folding Thermal Ground Sheet all crumpled up close by and laid it out neatly on the floor of the cave. Zag sat on it and set about the important task of mending the broken painting brush.

"And not before time, I must say," said Flewy indignantly.

"Shush, Zag needs to concentrate," said Lucy.

Flewy put on his nobody-likes-me look and trundled a little way deeper into the cave. "Waaark! I know when I'm not wanted," he called back.

Zag fumbled inside his Thingummajacket, taking out a roll of this, a strip of that and a tube of the other. He squeezed the tube over one of the broken ends, then fitted both pieces together. Immediately sparks all the colours of the rainbow flew in every direction. Briefly the painting brush glowed a bright silvery light that dazzled the eye. It was so strong that everybody had to look away from it.

"Sorry about that, I should have warned you," said Zag, proudly holding up the brush, which looked as if had never been broken.

"Let's find out if it works, shall we?" said Zag.

"Off now then, are ya? Back to where ya came from?" asked Eggbert.

"You must come with us," said Lucy.

"Wish I could, but I must finish the task that Eggna and I were sent to do. I owe her that much at least," said Eggbert sorrowfully.

"The waterfall sounds much louder all of a sudden," said William.

"That's not the waterfall," said Eggbert fearfully.

The intense bright light from the painting brush had been all that was needed to attract the attention of the searching Cameracraft. Flashing lights sped out of the gloom and headed straight towards the cave. The sound heard by William was the wind, and it was getting closer by the second.

Eggbert shouted, "They know where we are. Let's go! Let's go!" He flew to a cleft high up in the cave's wall and grabbed a small leathery pouch, which he hung around his neck. "Come on, do whatever you need to do. WE MUST BE QUICK! COME ON! THERE IS NO TIME TO LOSE!"

Gone Missing

Finding themselves safely back once more in Fisherman's Cottage, Zag could tell by the expressions on the twins' faces that they were hesitant to go to bed and risk missing out on further adventure.

Eggbert was engrossed in looking at the painting of Blot. "To think that we came here through that. How did ya do it?" he asked.

"Oh, it is just a thingummagadgetal invention of mine," said Zag modestly. "It would take rather a lot of explaining." Lucy caught Zag's attention by letting out a yawn. "Let's all have some sleep," he said, smiling, "then wake up to a good breakfast, to help us think clearly."

William was rather annoyed that Lucy had not kept her yawn to herself. Bed was definitely not part of his agenda, especially as he thought it unlikely his mum and dad would allow them to go back to Blot when they were told what had happened so far.

Lucy yawned again. "Come on, William." Looking around to say good-night, she asked, "Where's Flewy?"

"Sulking somewhere outside probably," said Eggbert.

"Hang on, I'll go and find him," said William, hoping to postpone going to bed until he could think of a better reason for staying up.

"Okay, but quickly and quietly," said Zag. "Remember, your mum and dad are fast asleep."

"How could we forget?" said Lucy with a grin, listening to the snoring duet coming from the bedroom above.

"Well, Eggbert," said Zag, "we promised to help you, but to do so I must fetch some Thingummagadgets from my barn before we return to Blot . . ." Zag looked expectantly at the lounge door. "That is, once Flewy graces us with his presence."

William hurried back into the lounge looking very concerned. "I can't find Flewy anywhere."

"Come to think of it, I haven't seen him since we came back," said Zag, beginning to look worried.

"Nor me," said Eggbert.

"Me neither," said Lucy. She gave her brother a knowing look, "Are you sure?"

"Of course I'm sure," he replied abruptly.

"Really, really, really sure?"

"Don't be stupid, Lucy," he answered crossly. "I'm being serious, you idiot."

Lucy lifted her eyebrows, said nothing and stared at him with a strong hint of disbelief.

Zag gave William a stern look of disapproval, fumbled in his Thingummajacket and pulled out a small disc, which he attached to the base of the painting brush. As he studied it closely, an anxious expression came over his face. "This tells me that four went and four came back. As Eggbert is here, that means Flewy is still on Blot, and all alone."

"I don't mean to worry ya further, but it is unlikely Flewy will be alone for long," said Eggbert.

"Surely he is bound to have stayed in the cave? I can't see Flewy going outside to the woods," Lucy reasoned.

"I agree. That should be the safest place for him," said Zag, hoping this would be the case.

"Actually it is not the safest place, especially if I am not there," said Eggbert. "Ally Catpone and his Mogsters prowl the island for Eraser."

"What would they do to him if they found him?" asked William.

"Eat him more than likely . . . Depends."

Zag cringed. "Depends on what?"

"How they feel. They would probably torture him first."

"Torture!" exclaimed William.

Lucy was in despair. "Oh, no, poor Flewy."

Zag had no doubts about what to do next. "We need Awoo," he said out loud.

Eggbert looked puzzled. "What's a Woo?"

"Awoo can see in the dark," replied Zag. "If Flewy has wandered off, Awoo will find him."

"Got ya. It's one of yar Thingummagadgets, isn't it?"

"No, Awoo is a good friend of ours," said Lucy.

Eggbert still didn't understand. "Er . . . Pass that one by me again."

Lucy tried to explain. "Awoo's an owl, he . . . "

"He lives in the barn with Zag," interrupted William.

Zag was restless. "Come on, Eggbert, we must leave for the barn straight away."

"What about us?" asked William, not wishing to miss out on anything.

Zag looked appealingly at Lucy. "Look, I'm sorry but you must go to bed. Eggbert, Awoo and I will find Flewy. Then, in the morning, we'll have fresh minds to solve the mystery of the sea-chest."

"So we must stay here?" asked Lucy.

"I'm afraid so," said Zag.

"All right, then."

William thought Lucy had given in far too

easily, but couldn't think of any way of changing Zag's mind. "Suppose that's it then!" he snapped, leaving to go upstairs.

Lucy shrugged. "Huh, boys!"

Zag smiled gently at her as she kissed him good-night and said, "Come back safely, Zag."

Zag and Eggbert crept out into the garden as quietly as possible. It was a still, clear night. The moon was full in the velvet sky.

"I'd forgotten the darkness could look so beautiful," whispered Eggbert. "I feel as if I could reach out and touch that star."

"That's the tail star of the Beamsurfer," whispered Zag.

"Beam . . . what ?"

"No time to explain. You will soon see what I mean." Zag quickly pulled off the Invisibilizing Sheet. Eggbert stood back in amazement at the sight of the Beamsurfer. Zag opened the door "Quickly, jump in." He checked they were fastened safely in their seats, set the co-ordinates and then surfed the beam back to his barn.

The Smelly Nightmare

"I knew it, I knew it, I knew it. If anyone was going to be accidentally left behind it was bound to be me," Flewy muttered angrily to himself as he plodded deeper into the cave to find a place to hide. "To think, to jolly well think, I didn't want to come here in the first place." He decided he had trundled far enough and stopped. "They had jolly well better come back for me, and jolly well quick, that's all I can jolly well say."

The flashing lights had long gone. The Eradicators, realizing that their prey had escaped when they saw the tubular green whirlwind of light, had abandoned their search.

Flewy comforted himself with the knowledge that Zag would not let him down, and anyway Zag had also promised Eggbert that he would come back to help him fight Eraser. He shuddered at the thought of all Eggbert had told them that evening. I must sit tight, he kept telling himself as he hid behind a rock. Zag's words ran through his mind: "We must keep ourselves under control to have any chance of getting out of here."

Shivering with the cold and damp, he resisted the temptation to return to the front of the cave to warm himself with the heat from the Heavy-duty Micro-folding Thermal Ground Sheet. It was far too big for him to drag even a short distance. In any case, he had no idea how to turn the crystal off and was afraid that if the Eradicators did come searching for him, they would see him at the front of the cave. He smiled to himself. "I bet even Zag doesn't know how to turn that crystal off," he thought. "That would be typical of him."

Flewy suddenly had that awful feeling he was no longer alone. He had heard various noises every now and again, but had put these down to the sounds of the waterfall and the water echoing as it dripped in the cave. Feeling the feathers on his back starting to quiver, he tried very hard to be brave, hoping that it would not be much longer before Zag and the others came to rescue him.

Hearing scuffling noises all around him, he crouched down as low as possible behind a rock. Five luminous green eyes stared at him out of the blackness and Flewy froze to his spot. One eye, all on its own, came closer towards him, bringing with it a horrible smell of foul breath.

"Uh . . . follow me, burdy, or uh . . . die," it breathed disgustingly.

Flewy had no choice but to follow the foul breath towards the front of the cave. As they got nearer to the glowing crystal, his worst nightmare was realized.

He was surrounded by three big, black cats, with no hope of escape. Each cat was dressed in what appeared to be a mixture of pirate and gangster clothes and was carrying a violin case. The suit jackets and trilby hats did not go at all well with the tights and swashbuckling boots.

"Are you for real?" said Flewy, in the faint hope that this was all a very bad dream.

Foul Breath stopped, casually turned around and stared at Flewy from under the brim of his low-slung trilby hat. The big cat's cruel look was emphasized by the deep, jagged scar that split his nose and deformed his face. One eye was covered over with a patch.

"Uh, allow me to weally intwoduce myself," he breathed slowly. "My name is . . . uh . . . uh . . ."

"Puss-in-Boots?" said Flewy, immediately wishing he hadn't.

"Uh . . . ALLY CATPONE, actually," said

Foul Breath disappointedly.

"Hey, Ally," shouted a very fat cat.

"Uh . . . what's der pwoblem, Gutwumble?" answered Foul Breath.

"I tink dis burdy is being cheeky."

Ally Catpone stuck his face right into Flewy's, breathing his foul breath. "UH . . . YOU BEING CHEEPY?"

"Not Cheepy, Ally! Cheeky," corrected Gutrumble.

Catpone stuck his face back into Flewy's and breathed, "DON'T BE CHIRPY."

"I certainly don't feel cheepy or chirpy," said Flewy, being cheeky.

"Hey, Ally. I gotta suggestion for my digestion."

"Yeah. What's dat, Guts?" breathed Foul Breath.

"Let's eat der burdy, before der eagle gets back."

"Uh ... twy a little patience, uh . . . Guts," said Foul Breath.

"Hey, Guts, cool it, uh?" said the third black cat, casually flicking his trilby into the air, then catching it playfully like an expert. His pointy white ears glowed eerily in the darkness. "I fink we ought ta ave sum fun wiv dis burdy on da beach first."

"Okay, Spooky, but I get der first bite," said Gutrumble, licking his slobbering lips.

"Hang on, you guys. I would hardly make a mouthful between you lot." Flewy noticed a horrible sight as Gutrumble waddled towards him: around the belt slung below the obscene, hanging gut was a row of dead rats tied by their tails. "Why bother eating me? Why not rats or something?" said Flewy desperately.

"Simple, cos we caught ya and too many rats give me wind, DAT'S WHY," said Gutrumble, untying one, then jerking off the head with one chewy bite.

Suddenly a long noise like a muffled machine gun rattled through the cave. Spooky caught Flewy by the scruff of the neck and they all dived for cover. Moments later a horrible smell filled the cave.

"Fffwarr, I wish yud keep off dose rats," shouted Spooky.

"Hey . . . Uh, Spooky . . . put da burdy in, uh . . . dis," said Ally Catpone, throwing the thermal ground sheet at him.

"Hang on, boss, I'm ratreev . . . ruttrevening . . . getting dis smelly sausages light," said Spooky, releasing the crystal from the rock with one powerful tug.

"Uh . . . huwwy up wiv dat burdy, will ya?" Catpone waved a grotty, razor-sharp claw, commanding all to follow him down to the beach.

The Note

William crept into Lucy's bedroom and found that she was staring out of the window.

"Shush, you'll wake up Mum and Dad."

"Did you see the Beamsurfer take off?" he asked.

"Yes;" said Lucy, still staring out of her window.

William sat next to her on the bed. "I can't sleep."

"Me neither. I keep thinking about poor Flewy."

"Me too."

Deep in thought, they both stared silently into the twinkling night sky.

"Sorry if I doubted you," said Lucy, putting her arm around William.

"I'm sorry too." He smiled. "Anyway, I've been thinking."

"I have as well and the answer is no," said Lucy.

"But we'd have more chance of saving Flewy because we could be there quicker."

"No."

"By the time Zag gets back here to go into the painting, we could be there and back with Flewy."

"But what if Flewy isn't in the cave?" asked Lucy.

William felt he was making progress. "He won't have left the cave. He'd be too scared."

Lucy was now gazing aimlessly into space. "That's true, I suppose." She suddenly realized what she had said. "I'm not listening to this. The answer is no!"

William had made up his mind. "I'll go on my own, then . . . " He got up from the bed and started to creep out of her bedroom . . . "cos I like Flewy a lot."

"That's unfair. So do I," said Lucy. "Oh, all right, then. Wait for me."

They made their way carefully along the landing. Being quiet was not easy, because most of the floorboards creaked. But practice had made near perfect. Apart from one or two mistakes, they knew where the creakiest floorboards lay.

One such mistake happened as they crept past their parents' bedroom. Their mother stirred and muttered something. Lucy and William froze in their tracks, scared they had woken her up, but luckily she remained asleep.

As Lucy moved on, the floor creaked underneath her. This time their dad let out a big sigh, then started to snore heavily. They waited a second to make extra sure, then as quickly and carefully as possible made their way downstairs into the kitchen.

"Cor, that was close," said William, very relieved.

Lucy looked thoughtful. The excitement and her sense of adventure were now getting the better of her. "I wonder . . ."

"Wonder what?"

"I wonder, if Zag was in such a hurry . . . whether he left anything behind."

"Like what?"

Lucy went towards the kitchen door. "Follow me, and be as quiet as a mouse."

William followed Lucy outside into the garden and up to the greenhouse. Suddenly Lucy was nowhere to be seen.

"Lucy, Lucy, where are you?"

"Shush, I'm over here," she giggled.

"Where?"

William froze as he saw Lucy's head coming towards him . . . no body, just a head. Before he could cry out, Lucy dropped the Invisibilizing Sheet.

"You frightened the life out of me. That was

stupid!"

"Couldn't resist it," she chuckled.

"Don't you ever do anything like that again."

"Sorry, I thought they might have left this behind."

"Hey, we could use it to hide ourselves, if we needed to," William suggested.

"Exactly! That's what I thought," said Lucy, bundling it back to the kitchen.

William fetched a small rucksack from the cupboard under the stairs and they stuffed the Invisibilizing Sheet inside. Not being able to see it created a little difficulty, but with a few muffled giggles this was soon overcome.

"We'd better wear something warm," said Lucy, carefully fastening the rucksack.

"Look, Mum left our track-suits in the basket by the boiler ready for washing," said William, putting them to his nose. "They don't smell too bad. We can wear them over our pyjamas."

They double-checked they had everything, put on their slightly niffy track-suits and crept into the lounge.

William stood by the side of the picture, painting brush in hand, ready to leave. "We're all set to go," he said excitedly.

"Just wait a minute," said Lucy.

"What for?" asked William impatiently.

"We must leave a note in case Zag, Eggbert and Awoo return before we get back." Lucy went over to her father's desk and found a Post-it pad and pen.

"Hurry up, will you?" said William. The last thing he wanted was for the others to arrive back and spoil his fun.

Lucy quickly wrote the note and stuck it on the lounge door. She stood next to William and he drew the magic circle around them. He touched the painting with the brush and in a flash of green light they were gone.

The New Recruit

"Amazing craft, absolutely amazing," Eggbert kept repeating as he watched Zag busy himself with picking up some things, talking to himself, then putting other things back down. "Will ya have enough room in the Beamsurfer for all that stuff?" he queried.

"It will all have to go into my Thingummajacket first because I haven't had time to fit a Miniaturization Sifter to the Beamsurfer." Zag lifted his fez and scratched his head. "I must do that some time."

Eggbert heard a noise coming from the top corner of the barn and went to investigate. The final stage of loading the Beamsurfer was suddenly interrupted by a lot of scuffling and a few feathers coming out of the dimly lit top corner of the hayloft.

"I say, do you mind, old chap? These are my private quarters, so go away!"

"Sorry, it's just I thought ya might have been an intruder."

"Get off me, you, you, you . . ."

"Eagle," said Eggbert, as he tried to make amends by brushing the straw and dust off Awoo.

"Eagle? EAGLE! H. . .H. . .HELP!" shouted Awoo, as he took off in fright, not looking where he was going. He crashed into the Beamsurfer, landing in an undignified heap at Zag's feet.

"Are you all right, Awoo?" asked Zag.

"Th. . .there is an eagle in here. A b. . .blinking great BIG eagle," said Awoo, picking himself up and looking rather dazed.

"Meet Eggbert," Zag said with a chuckle.

"Sorry, didn't mean to startle ya," said Eggbert, landing beside them.

"Eggbert? You mean that fierce-looking lump is called Eggbert?" said Awoo, brushing himself down with his wing.

Zag grinned mischievously. "Don't laugh," he advised.

"Would I dare?" said Awoo.

"Hey, don't ya owls have excellent eyesight in the dark?" enquired Eggbert.

"Naturally, old chap. We owls are renowned for that quality." Awoo stuck out his chest with pride. "Just one of many, of course."

"Of course. Then if ya have a mind to, I am sure ya could be of great help to us," said Eggbert, looking at him convincingly.

Awoo was persuaded, because when you see an eagle the size of Eggbert, you tend to want to appear helpful.

"Now, let me show our new recruit the inside of this splendid craft," said Eggbert, putting a large wing around Awoo.

Zag gave a knowing wink to Eggbert as he followed them aboard the Beamsurfer. He settled down in his seat and set the co-ordinates. "Fasten your seat-belts," he said, checking everybody was secure. With a press of a button and pull of a lever, they surfed the beam to Fisherman's Cottage.

"Now isn't this amazing?" said Eggbert. "What'ya think, Awoo? Isn't it amazing? Makes ya want to hand in ya wings, doesn't it?"

"Terrrrriiiiiffffic," said Awoo, as the craft did a tack manoeuvre.

"Whey hey, one more time, Zag," shouted Eggbert.

"Excuse me, Mr Eggbert, but you still have not explained how I can help you," said Awoo.

"Sorry, pal, I got carried away." Eggbert chuckled at his own joke.

Awoo laughed, thinking this the appropriate response under the circumstances. "So how can I help you, old chap?"

"Well, you see, it is like this. We have mislaid a seagull called Flewy."

"FLEWY? That irritable excuse for a seagull! He should never have been laid in the first place."

"That's the one. Ya obviously know him."

"Know him?" said Awoo. "Please, leave him wherever he is. It will be far more peaceful for everybody, believe me."

"We can't do that," said Zag, as he twiddled the joystick. "Coming in to land. Make sure your seat-belts are fastened."

Before Eggbert could explain further, the Beamsurfer landed with a whisper in the back garden of Fisherman's Cottage, once again just missing the greenhouse.

"Quiet please, so we don't wake up the family," said Zag.

They all got out of the craft and Zag started scrambling around the garden. "I can't seem to find the Invisibilizing Sheet." Zag fumbled inside his Thingummajacket and pulled out his Invizibilizer Detector. "Strange, it has gone missing."

"Maybe it's blown away," said Eggbert.

"Never mind. I have more in my Thingummajacket," said Zag, not wanting to waste time. "Come on, we must go back to the painting inside the cottage and rescue Flewy."

The Mogster Pirates

Lucy and William were very surprised to find themselves on the beach back in Blot, but quickly took cover behind an upturned rowing boat.

"I thought we would be brought back to the cave, or at least somewhere close," said William. "We'll never find it from here."

"We are very lucky we didn't land in the sea," Lucy said, looking at the waves pounding the rocks nearby.

William shuddered at the thought of it.

Lucy checked that the painting brush was safe and all in one piece. "Maybe we should go back," she said.

"What if they've seen our note and are already here looking for us?" said William.

"If Zag is on the island, he won't leave without finding us," Lucy reasoned.

"And if we did go back, we could end up going

to and fro, missing each other," said William.

"It's all your fault, William," said Lucy abruptly. "We should never have come back to Blot."

"You needn't have come," he replied angrily.

"It's easy for you to say that now," said Lucy huffily.

"Oh yeah . . . I didn't force you."

"You did. You said I didn't care about Flewy."

"I said no such thing," said William, trying to remember what he actually had said.

"Anyway, we can't just sit here and argue. We need to work out what we should do for the best," said Lucy.

Fate was already beginning to make up their minds for them. A glowing light erratically bounced its way high up in the distant darkness, occasionally disappearing and then reappearing.

"Did you see that light?" said William.

"What light?" said Lucy, trying to follow the direction of William's pointing finger.

"I think it's a lantern. Look, there it is again."

This time Lucy saw the glow. They both watched the pinpoint glow become bigger as it hopped and skipped towards the beach.

"It's coming in our direction," said Lucy.

"It may be Zag," said William excitedly.

"Or it could be someone coming for this boat."

Lucy grabbed her brother's hand. "Quickly, we need to find another hiding place just in case."

They ran a short distance up the beach and crept behind clump of palm trees which seemed to have withered in despair at their bleak surroundings. Holding each other close, they watched the glowing light float in the darkness towards the upturned boat. Occasionally it would stop, and the sound of raucous laughter could be heard. Eventually three large, shadowy figures, carrying the light, reached the upturned boat. They were so close that Lucy and William hardly dared breathe.

"Uh . . . okay . . . uh . . . let's play tap and fly," said Catpone.

"Den eats, eh, boss? Dis smell of sausages is making my stomach feel cut off from my troat," said Gutrumble, as he placed the glowing light on the sand.

"Look! Th . . . they have the crystal and th . . . they're the size of panthers!" gasped William.

"Shush, they might hear you," said Lucy, trying hard to keep calm.

"Do you think they're pirates?" William whispered.

Lucy could not believe her eyes. "They look very odd to me. Only gangsters and orchestras carry violin cases."

"They're definitely not an orchestra," replied William.

Lucy and William watched intently as a large cat opened a violin case and took out a cutlass. It thrust the sword up to the hilt in the sand and tied a piece of thin rope to the handle.

"Gimmee der, uh . . . burdy," shouted Catpone.

"Wid pleasure, boss," said Spooky, handing over the bundle.

Catpone crouched down, unwrapped something and tied it to the end of the rope.

"Flewy!" said William, so shocked he couldn't keep his voice down.

Lucy pulled William back down under the cover of the fallen palm trees.

"What's wiv der noise?" said Gutrumble.

The cats stood deathly still. Lucy and William froze. The next few seconds seemed to last hours.

"Uh . . . okay, let's get on wiv da game," said Catpone. "Uh . . . Guts, explain da wules to da burdy."

"Come on, fellas," said Flewy weakly. "You don't want to do this really."

Gutrumble bent down towards him. "Da rules are simple. We kick ya, den ya fly in circles cos yar tied to dis rope. Den we twy to knock ya down wiv our paws. Den when all dat's over, I EAT YA! Got it?"

"WE EAT YA!" said Spooky.

"Yeah, sorry, Spooky, WE eat ya," said Gutrumble, sounding a bit disappointed.

"Don't you lot ever think? If you make me fly about, I will lose weight and there will be even less of me to eat," said Flewy desperately.

"Dat . . . uh . . . burdy's being cheepy again," said Catpone.

"Cheeky," corrected Gutrumble.

"Uh . . . whatever," said Catpone.

"Anyways, boss, dere will be a lot less of dis burdy when he's been eaten," said Gutrumble, fondly patting his fat, ugly gut and sorting out some excess wind.

"Fffwarr! I told ya, keep off dem rats, didun I?" said Spooky.

"Having no food makes me wude," burped Gutrumble.

"Dat sounds like, uh . . .weal poultry, Guts," said Catpone, making double sure the knot was firm around Flewy's leg.

"Dat was poetry, boss. Chickens, dere poultry," Gutrumble corrected.

"Uh . . . even I know dis burdy's not a chicken . . . ya fink I'm stoopid or sumfink?" Catpone picked Flewy up from the sand and put his foul breath in Flewy's face. " Uh . . . say sum poultry den, burdy."

Flewy thought quickly, then:

"Your breath's so smelly it makes me sick.
You're really ugly and extremely thick."

"Dat's not good cos it's rude. So now I'm gonna eat ya," burped Gutrumble.

Lucy and William knew they had to think quickly. Suddenly a rumbling sound could be heard in the distance and a strong breeze began to rustle through the fallen palm trees. A rush of wind blew up a mini sandstorm as a lone bright flashing light circled in the thick cloud above. For a brief moment a ray of sunshine peeped through a hole in the cloud made by a Cameracraft as it cut its way through and came to land nearby on the beach.

"What da dey want now?" said Gutrumble, who had been just about to use Flewy as a football.

The Discoveries

Meanwhile, back at Fisherman's Cottage, Zag, Eggbert and Awoo had crept into the lounge. They were anxious to rescue Flewy and all set to enter the painting. Zag reached into his Thingummajacket and pulled out the painting brush he had repaired in Eggbert's cave. He was about to whisk them into the picture when he paused. "On second thoughts, I think we ought to take both painting brushes with us."

"Good idea," said Eggbert. "Ya never know. Best to have a back-up."

Zag went and opened the highly polished carrying case, but was surprised to find it empty. "It must be around here somewhere. That is, unless Lucy and William have it upstairs."

The three of them quickly searched the lounge, but it was nowhere to be found. Eggbert picked up a piece of paper that had fallen down by the door and read it. "Hey, Zag! Take a look at this," he said, handing over the note for Zag to read. "Sorry, pal, we've now got an even bigger problem."

Dear Zag and all,
Gone to find Flewy. See you in Eggbert's cave.
Lots of love,
Lucy and William xxxx

Putting his hands to his face, Zag sighed deeply.

"What if their parents wake up?" said Eggbert.

"We must not panic," said Zag. "At least the time we return will still be exactly the same time as we leave for Blot."

"Blot? Arrive back the same time as we leave?" said Awoo. "I think I need a thorough explanation."

Zag's face suddenly lit up. He rushed across to the bookshelf and took out a maritime volume called *Unsolved Mysteries of the High Seas*. "I am sure it's in here somewhere." He put on his half-rimmed glasses and quickly flicked through the pages. "There we are. I knew it." He pointed to a picture of a beautiful tropical island that looked like Blot. Zag read out the words beneath the picture: "THE SECRET ISLAND. An old tale of the sea tells of a mysterious, cut-throat pirate called Captain Terry Bull, who sailed the seven seas in his black galleon, the *Sea Err*.

He plundered unfortunate ships that crossed his path, then mysteriously vanished into a dark, grey mist it is said to this very island.

"Odd name for a ship. 'Err' can mean to stray off course," said Zag, thoughtfully placing the book on the coffee table beside him. "Mmm, change around the letters S E A E R R and they spell ERASER."

Awoo had put on his trying-to-be-wise look, as he watched Eggbert shuffle nervously around the lounge.

Deep in thought, Zag didn't notice the lack of contribution from Eggbert or Awoo. "Then where does Captain Terry Bull fit in?" he said, thinking out loud. "That's it! Captain Terry Bull . . . Terrible," he said excitedly. "Captain Terrible is . . . Eraser the Terrible. The name has been misinterpreted as the tale's been passed on from one person to the other."

"Well, of course!" said Awoo, whose completely vacant expression spoke volumes.

Zag tried to explain. "The *Sea Err* is the ship I saw when I was out fishing with Mike and the twins."

"Fishing . . . Eraser . . . Not a clue what you're on about," said Awoo, deciding none of this nonsense was scientific enough to exercise his brain.

Eggbert shuffled apprehensively. "Look, ya must understand, it's difficult for me to trust anybody, but now I must show ya something."

"If you know something that can help us save Flewy and the twins," said Zag firmly, "you must tell us."

"Ya must believe that I am trusting ya with the true meaning of for ever and beyond."

"For ever and beyond?" asked Awoo, thinking this was a far better quality of information to pass on and help him look wise.

"Infinity," answered Zag.

Eggbert took off the leathery pouch from around his neck and produced a stone. Astonished to find that it was glowing a deep luminous blue, he gasped, "Ya must have the Orb of Brilliance!"

"Wait here," said Zag, and he crept out to the kitchen.

"Don't ask me, old chap. Quite frankly I know nothing," said Awoo to Eggbert.

Eggbert gave him a knowing sort of look.

"About this, I mean," said Awoo indignantly.

Zag returned, holding the silvery orb that he had found in the sea-chest earlier that evening.

Eggbert's heart raced at the sight of it. "How did ya get this?"

"For the moment, let's just say by chance, on a fishing trip," smiled Zag, as he opened the orb. The stone inside was no longer misty grey but glowed a luminous red. The two stones fitted together perfectly, and their luminosity increased dramatically.

"As ya can see, the Orb of Brilliance holds a sphere made up of four interlocking stones," explained Eggbert excitedly. "The Red Stone of Skill, Blue Stone of Inspiration, Green Stone of Imagination and the White Stone of Genius."

Zag stroked his beard. "It appears we have the stones of Skill and Inspiration. So where are the other two?"

"Eraser's got them . . . well, he has now." Eggbert looked sad. "He wears the Stone of Genius around his neck and Eggna had the Stone of Imagination in her talons when she was captured."

"Well, haven't we stumbled into something?" commented Awoo, not realizing the enormity of the understatement he had made.

"What ya may find hard to understand . . . "

"Hmm," Awoo interrupted, his trying-to-be-wise look fixed on Eggbert, "unlikely, old chap, but nevertheless carry on."

"The whole Orb of Brilliance must be returned to the Master of the Galaxy. It was he who sent Eggna and me to help Astral, the Master's most trusted Defender, recover it."

"This Astral fellow must be more on your wave-length," said Awoo, trying to find the easy way out.

"Best bet, I reckon, is that you get him to assist you, old chap."

"He's betrayed us." Eggbert sighed. "Ya see, it is Astral who now calls himself Artless the Heartless."

"As Eraser only has part of the Orb, how does he still have the power to mess everything up?" asked Zag.

"Ya see, when Eraser had the complete Orb, he created his tools of power, like his ship and Cameracraft, et cetera, et cetera. But now the Orb and stones are separated, even he's on borrowed time . . . just like all of us."

Awoo suddenly paid attention "What do you mean, old chap?"

Eggbert had noticed Awoo's propensity to drift off.

"Which bit?"

"The 'just like all of us' bit will do," said Awoo, raising an eyebrow.

"Yud betta listen hard, pal. If the Orb remains separated everything there is, including him and us, will become a thick, black, sticky, gooey mess."

Zag repeated the inscription. " 'Protect within each fiery stone locked as one, each never alone.' So that's what it means."

It was as if the Stones of Skill and Inspiration were boosting Zag's already clever mind. His brain was in overdrive as he reasoned out loud. "If Eraser's ship can disappear and reappear, there must be other ways of getting to Blot. There must be a way I can use the Beamsurfer."

Awoo paced about, battling to look wise, but his brain was rather immune to such wonders.

Zag suddenly picked up the book from the coffee table. "Okay, I have a plan, so you must listen carefully," he said.

Eggbert looked very relieved, but Awoo seemed a little concerned about what this plan might entail.

"As we have only one brush, my plan is to take the Beamsurfer to Blot, as a back-up. By scanning the picture from this book into the Beamsurfer's Direction Locator, I should be able to find a beam that will take me through the Galaxy of Ideas, into the World of Creativity and then, hopefully, to Blot."

"How can ya do that?" asked Eggbert. "Blot's covered in darkness."

"By using the painting brush," Zag answered. He quickly explained how it worked, concluding, " . . . so you take Awoo into the painting, then use the brush to paint a large hole in the dark cloud to allow the   sunlight through."

"Hold on a minute," said Awoo.

"Don't ya trust me?" asked Eggbert.

"Why, silly old me, of course I do, old chap."

Zag pointed to an area of the woods on the painting. "It is very important you touch the painting right here, because the painting doesn't show the entrance to the cave. You must avoid that waterfall."

"Prime spot. Much closer to my cave than where I first found ya."

"Okay, listen carefully," said Zag. "It's vital you let me take off before you enter the painting, otherwise you risk restricting me in this particular time zone."

Eggbert nodded. "Where will you land?" he asked.

"Inside the entrance to the cave. It's big enough to take the Beamsurfer. The crystal we left jammed in the rock will guide the Beamsurfer behind the curtain of the waterfall." Zag was anxious to go as quickly as possible. "Okay, so are we all ready?"

Awoo nervously fluttered his wings.

"Stick close to me, pal, ya'll be all right," said Eggbert.

"One final thing," said Zag, about to leave. "Keep clear of the cave's entrance. We don't want any accidents." He smiled, "Oh, and the best of luck."

"Same," said Eggbert.

"See you soon, old chap . . . I hope," said Awoo.

Zag took the book containing the picture of Blot

and crept out to the garden. Eggbert and Awoo watched through the window as the Beamsurfer disappeared like a burst of stardust into the clear night sky.

"Okay, pal, time for us to go," said Eggbert, picking up the painting brush. "Stand real close to me, cos I don't want to leave ya behind."

"Perish the very thought, old chap."

Eggbert drew the magic circle, touched the painting with the tip of the brush on the chosen spot, and they vanished in a flash of green light.

All Caught Up

Lucy and William looked on quietly from behind the clump of withered palm trees, not daring to make a sound. Close by, the Mogsters stood in a group by the dinghy, watching a dark figure climb out of the sleek oval-shaped Cameracraft and walk over to them.

"Might have guessed," said the Eradicator arrogantly.

"Uh . . . what's da pwoblem?"

"The problem is, Catpone, that light! Where did you get it?" The Eradicator picked up the crystal.

"Uh . . . is dat what all dis fuss is about?"

William whispered to Lucy. "Maybe we could grab Flewy now while they're not looking."

"What are you doing with that seagull and where did it come from?" asked the Eradicator, drawing everyone's attention back to Flewy.

Lucy and William had already lost their opportunity.

"Uh . . . questions and more questions. Tell him, Guts," said Catpone.

"We dunno der burdy's history, but we're gonna eat it anyways," belched Gutrumble.

"Why have you not reported all of this?" said the Eradicator firmly.

"What's t'report bout eating a burdy?" burped Gutrumble.

The Eradicator quickly lost his temper. "TAKE THE SEAGULL TO YOUR DIRTY LITTLE SHIP AND INTERROGATE IT!"

"Uh . . .what's interrogut?" asked Catpone.

"We ask der burdy questions, den eat it, boss," replied Gutrumble.

"You do NOTHING more than I have ordered. I will report this to Eraser and he will want to meet this seagull. IS THAT CLEAR?"

"Dat means we definitely can't eat it. We gotta qwestion it," said Spooky.

"Who wants to talk to food?" grumbled Gutrumble, checking out the dead rats around his belly.

The Eradicator looked at the crystal in his hand. "Eraser will be very interested in this smelly thing as well," he added, keeping hold of it.

Suddenly a huge beam of sunlight broke through a large hole in the sky. It was as if a very bright light had suddenly been turned on in a dark room, taking everybody by surprise.

Because the twins' eyes were used to daylight, they recovered far more quickly than the others. They took their chance and grabbed Flewy, but the rope on the cutlass held him fast. Lucy unravelled the Invisibilizing Sheet and covered them with it as William pulled the cutlass from out of the sand. Under the cover of the sheet, they scurried up the beach, carrying Flewy still tied to the cutlass.

"Da burdy's gone!" shouted Gutrumble.

The daylight worked against Lucy and William. Their scuffled footprints could be seen in the sand, allowing the Eradicator and Mogsters to chase after them. The Mogsters, apart from one, got to them first, the Eradicator second, Gutrumble third. William, Lucy and Flewy were surrounded, and Spooky pounced around, eventually landing on top of them. It took no time for the Invisibilizing Sheet to be torn apart by his sharp claws, exposing the frightened contents.

William immediately swung the cutlass and slashed the thin rope that held Flewy. He put up a brave defence as Gutrumble made a grab at Flewy. Summoning all his strength, William thumped Gutrumble's fat gut with the flat of the cutlass. Flewy saw his chance and took off into the air.

"Take these two kids back to your ship and don't let them escape. Eraser will want to interrogate them," the Eradicator ordered. "I must recapture that seagull, then report back to Eraser."

"Uh . . .what happens if dey ave other twicks?" asked Catpone.

As he rushed off to his Cameracraft, the Eradicator shouted back, "If those kids escape, you will all be put in Collage."

"Uh . . . okay . . . uh . . . uh . . . don't waste time. Uh, Spooky, uh . . . tie up dose kids," Catpone ordered.

The Mogsters dragged their dinghy towards the edge of the sea. Tied to a leash firmly held by Spooky, the twins reluctantly followed behind. Looking up in the sky, they saw the desperate, wobbly flight of Flewy. Spooky gave a strong tug on the rope, which made Lucy wince with pain and nearly pulled her to the ground. "Yah fwend's a gonner, so move yuhselves, yer little brats."

"Hey! That's my sister you're hurting," shouted William.

"SHURRUP! Dat's nuffink to what's gonna 'appen." The big cat pointed to the Cameracraft in the sky as it teasingly hovered above Flewy.

Flewy's heart pounded in his chest. He began to lose height as exhaustion from his recent ordeals took its toll. He could see the waterfall and, with a final effort, he desperately tried to make the height of the cliff, but it was too late. Flewy's eyes closed with the intensity of the flash from the Cameracraft as it captured his true meaning in a prismatran.

"Dat's a waste of good food," said Gutrumble miserably. He pushed Lucy and William into the dinghy, and they all set off for the Mogsters' galleon, the *Mobsea Dick*.

Beamsurfing

The Beamsurfer was working to perfection, surfing the galactic beams that bounced off the smooth, silver craft into a cosmic sea of beautiful colours.

Zag stared uneasily at the large monitor, then checked the time indicator on the control panel. All sorts of confused images were flashing across the screen, but none looked even remotely like the island of Blot.

"This is hopeless," he said out loud .

He slowed the Beamsurfer down to a hover and pressed the button that opened the cover of the observation window. It slid neatly aside, revealing the wonder of the universe in all its brilliant glory. The Beamsurfer slowly rotated clockwise.

He let out a deep sigh as he took in the enormity of his task. "All those stars. Even if I could visit all that I can see, I would still find more, and more, and more."

A thought came to him like a bolt from the blue. "I'm not looking for a star. I'm looking for a window of light. Blot is covered in a thick black cloud, but Eggbert will have cut a hole in it."

His mind raced with excitement as he talked to himself. "The direction finder must have been confused because the picture from the book showed a beautiful tropical island. But that island does not exist in terms of light. What does exist is a black mass with a hole of bright sunlight, and if Eggbert has managed to cut that hole, the only part of the island that can be seen is where the sun is shining on the waterfall in front of the cave."

Zag studied the picture of Blot in the direction finder and focused the scanner on the area of the cliffs and the waterfall that led to the cave. To his delight the big screen clearly showed the correct destination. Heaving a sigh of relief, he carefully fed in the new co-ordinates, then put the Beamsurfer on automatic mode.

In a split second he was beamsurfing in the Galaxy of Ideas. He left the observation cover open, captivated by the breathtaking sight of fiery comets, all colours of the rainbow, shooting across the galactic void outside the craft. Some chased and crashed into huge, porridge-like blobs, exploding them into clouds of gooey mist. Incredibly, they survived the impact, shooting onwards to complete their dazzling journey.

"Now that's a bit strange," Zag thought, noticing that every comet and blob was travelling in exactly the same direction as the Beamsurfer. It was as if an extremely powerful magnet of some sort was drawing everything towards it. A radiant blue planet came into view, shining out of the darkness and overwhelming the galaxy with its awesome beauty. It looked exactly how he had imagined the World of Creativity to be, except it was marred by a distinctive black spot.

Zag adjusted the craft's powerful telescope and checked his position on the screen. It still showed the cliffs and the waterfall. "This must be it," he said out loud. Nearing the planet's atmosphere, he closed the observation window and switched on the monitor linked to the telescope. He could clearly see a pinprick of light in the middle of the black spot. The porridge-like blobs devoured the fiery comets that tried to take the same course, then finally swarmed like gigantic bees into the black spot. "So that's how the thick gooey cloud builds up," he muttered.

As the Beamsurfer took up the final stage of its journey, the black spot grew to an enormous blot and the pinprick became a narrow tunnel of light. Numbers appeared on the small screen and a green light flashed. The Beamsurfer was on course to pass through the hole in the thick black cloud. Zag locked into the crystal that he had left in Eggbert's cave and switched to manual flight control. He opened the cover of the observation window, and to his surprise found himself heading directly for a huge, sinister-looking galleon with tall black sails.

The Beamsurfer hovered just below the dark cloud covering Blot. Zag trained the telescope on the bow of the ship. "The *Sea Err*," he said to himself. "So this is where you disappeared to!"

Circling the ship slowly, he saw the long open deck on its port side. Zag could hardly believe his eyes. "How amazing. It looks like a cross between a galleon and a . . . I don't believe it . . . an aircraft carrier!"

For the first time, Zag had the opportunity to see the Cameracraft properly. One had just landed and was manoeuvring into position at the end of a row of five others. Focusing more closely on the flight deck, he clearly saw the smooth, tail-less stingray shape, the telescopic lens at the nose of the craft and the silvery, diamond-shaped window, which Zag rightly concluded was a powerful flashlight.

He watched intently as an Eradicator climbed out of the Cameracraft to be greeted by two other figures, one of which hopped up and down in a frenzy, then walked swiftly away. Moments later the *Sea Err* sailed off at an incredible speed towards a much smaller black galleon that was anchored just off the coast. Having been totally absorbed in all he had seen, it only then dawned on Zag that the Beamsurfer had locked on to the *Sea Err* and not Eggbert's cave. He realized that the crystal must be somewhere on board the galleon and began to fear the worst. "If that is the case, has everybody been captured?" he said to himself, as he pushed the joystick forward.

The Beamsurfer swooped to follow the coast-line as Zag searched for the waterfall, but his presence had not passed unnoticed.

Artless ordered another Cameracraft into action. "Follow that craft. Don't let it see you. Don't shoot at it. I only want to know where it lands." He watched the Cameracraft take off, momentarily ignoring the Eradicator, who had just landed and was now waiting patiently beside him. "So what precious gifts are you bearing for Eraser?" he asked sarcastically.

"I've captured the image of a seagull, Sar," came the reply.

Artless sniffed at the air as he took the Eradicator below deck to Eraser's cabin. "Have you been eating greasy sausages, by any chance?"

Rendezvous

Eggbert had carried out a thorough search of his cave while Awoo waited patiently, trying to ignore the smell.

"Well, Flewy's not here," said Eggbert.

"Easy to deduce," said Awoo with an air of pomposity. "I've already told you that, old chap. It's far too quiet. He'd drown even the noise of that waterfall."

"I know what ya mean," Eggbert said with a grin. "Even so, he could have been injured."

"If that were the case, he would have made even more noise."

Now that a hole in the cloud had been cut with the painting brush, the cave was partially lit by rays of sunlight. Eggbert peered into the half-light and hoped that Zag would have sufficient room to land the Beamsurfer. It was then that he realized . . . "The crystal has gone! It was jammed between those rocks."

"What crystal?" asked Awoo, proving he hadn't

really been listening to Zag's plan.

Eggbert did not answer. He was too busy thinking out loud. "Only those Mogsters would have been strong enough to prise it from the rock."

Awoo frowned. "What on earth . . . or wherever we are . . . are you talking about?"

Eggbert could see no sign of a struggle, no scattering of seagull feathers. "Wait here, Awoo. Hopefully Zag won't be long."

"Where the dickens are you going?"

"To circle the *Mobsea Dick* . . . I'll be back soon."

Awoo's face was a complete blank. "Eh . . .? What . . .? Who . . .? But . . ."

Eggbert had already taken off and was heading out to sea.

"Uh . . . keep wowing der boat, lads. Der daylight's weal good." Catpone was enjoying the novelty of being able to look at the sea. "Uh . . . hey, look at dat shoal of delphiniums," said Catpone.

"School of dolphins," corrected Gutrumble.

"Whatever," said Catpone, with a thoughtful expression on his scarred face. "Uh . . . edificated fish?"

"Dere not fish in da true sense of da word," said Gutrumble.

"Uh . . . don't be stoopid, Guts," said Catpone.

"Hey, Guts, look at dat eagle up in da sky," said Spooky.

"Now dat's what I call lunch," said Gutrumble.

"Uh . . . keep, uh . . . ya conce . . . concen . . . concentr, on where ya wowing, Guts," said Catpone.

It was too late. They crashed into the port side of the *Mobsea Dick*.

Eggbert circled the galleon once more, then flew off into the distance. The sight of him greatly encouraged the twins. They felt that help was at hand.

A white cat peered over the side of the ship and purred out loud, "What's wiv der sunlight? It's making der garbage pongy."

"Don't knock it, Legs," shouted Gutrumble, clumsily grasping the rope ladder.

"Uh . . . did ya see dose edificated fish?" asked Catpone.

"What'ya on about now, Catpone?" said Legs Diamonte, closely studying her painted nails.

"Uh . . . dat's my gal," laughed Catpone into William's face.

"Your breath stinks," said William crossly.

"And to think we were worried about wearing our slightly niffy track-suits," Lucy said indignantly.

"Uh . . . don't be, uh . . . cheepy," said

Catpone, pushing the twins towards the rope ladder.

"Make sure dey don't twy and jump off, Spooks," shouted Gutrumble from the top of the rope ladder.

"Mind it, Guts. Concentwate on yuh own pwoblems," shouted Spooky impatiently, as he watched the alarming sight of Gutrumble hauling his bulk on to the festering, slime-ridden *Mobsea Dick*.

Glancing away from her eyeliner mirror, Legs purred, "Oooh, look at that."

Catpone joined them on deck, looked and took a deep gulp of fresh air. "Uh . . . and j. . .just w. . .when I fought evwyfink was getting up noses."

"Coming up roses, boss," Gutrumble corrected.

"Ewaser gets wight up my pwitty little nose," remarked Legs, delicately dabbing it with powder, as they watched the *Sea Err* sailing swiftly towards them. "Anyways, who uh dese two?"

"I'm William and this is my sister, Lucy."

"Why yuh wearing wopes?" Legs enquired.

"Uh . . . Legs . . . dere sausages," interrupted Catpone.

"Hostages, boss," Gutrumble corrected.

"Pity, cos dey look like nice kids." Legs snapped shut her powder compact. "A bit weserved, but nice."

"Uh . . . don't go getting bwoody, Legs," said Catpone.

"Der word dat spwings tuh mind is moody," grumbled Gutrumble, thinking about Eraser as the *Sea Err* manoeuvred close to.

A manic grin spread its evil across Eraser's scrawny face as he looked out of his cabin window at the *Mobsea Dick* and listened to the splash of the *Sea Err* dropping anchor.

"You may leave us now," he ordered the Eradicator. "One of your better choices," he said to Artless, as the Eradicator closed the cabin door behind him.

"Well, we've captured an eagle, a seagull, a crystal and now these two kids," said Artless. "Not bad, eh?"

"NOT BAD? We still need to find the missing stones, not a smelly crystal," Eraser raved. "AND WHY is that hole in the cloud taking so much time to seal up?"

"It is closing up," said Artless, pointing out of

the cabin window.

"Not quickly enough!" Eraser snarled, peering angrily through his pig-like eyes. He went over to his splendid mirror to preen himself and readjust the ruffles on his shirt. Suddenly his shirt lit up, sending him into fits of insane giggles. "It's glowing, the stone is glowing," he cackled, bouncing up and down like a demented ostrich, while holding up the white Stone of Genius between his crooked thumb and bony forefinger.

Artless looked amazed. "The Orb must be on this island!"

"Of course it is." Eraser wrinkled his hooked nose and snarled. "Use your brains. It must be on the craft that we had followed."

Artless remained cool. "I wonder if those two brats on the *Mobsea Dick* know anything about this. I will slowly torture them with rat bites and they will soon tell us all we need to know."

Eraser became excited. "Yes. YES! Music to my ears."

"Then I will put them in Collage before their wounds heal so that they hurt for ever."

"Yes. YES! YEEEEESSS! You can be soooo cruel!" said Eraser, hopping from leg to leg gleefully.

"Then I will torture the seagull and that stupid eagle over a roasting spit, and put them part-done into

Collage."

Eraser picked at his nose confidently. "Yes. YES! YEEEESS! Now we're cooking!" He excitedly rolled his horrible excavation into a tacky ball between his fingers, and flicked it at a nearby goblet. "Soon the Orb will be back in my . . . uh . . . our possession and I . . . I mean we, will become the masters of Creation itself."

Having wound themselves up, they rushed on to

the deck like hooligans, shoving and kicking out of their way anything and everything remotely in their path.

"COME ON, MOVE IT!" Eraser screamed impatiently at his crew, as he and Artless waited for them to ready the tender that would row them across to the *Mobsea Dick*.

All at Sea

Zag had not noticed the pursuing Cameracraft. Without the aid of the crystal, his concentration had been focused on negotiating the Beamsurfer through the precarious gap between the cliff and the raging waterfall. One small mistake, and he and the craft could easily be sucked into the flailing mass of water and smashed against the rock face.

With great skill he landed inside the mouth of the cave. His relief at finding Eggbert and Awoo safe was soon cut short as he learned that Flewy had not been found and that the twins had been captured.

"Maybe Flewy was in the bottom of the dinghy and I didn't see him," said Eggbert, not knowing that Flewy had suffered a similar fate to that of Eggna.

"It is very worrying to think that the *Sea Err* is anchored alongside the *Mobsea Dick*," said Zag.

"I could go and see if Flewy and the twins have been transferred to the *Sea Err*," suggested Eggbert.

"Much too risky in the sunlight. You're bound

to be spotted. Eraser would launch his Cameracraft and shoot you before you had time to blink," said Zag. "It would be far safer to work under the cover of darkness."

Awoo became aware of the fact that he had suddenly become the centre of attention. "Flying over land is one thing, old chap, but over the sea is another."

"I know it's a lot to ask, but will you do it?" said Zag.

Awoo weighed up the situation in his mind. "Yes, I will do it . . . I must be a twit after all."

"No, I think you'll find brave is the word," said Zag.

Awoo puffed out his chest, feeling that he had become a very important part of the team. "How far are they out to sea, Eggbert, old chap? I will need some directions, you know."

"The *Mobsea Dick* is anchored in a cove just around the coastline from here, just over half a mile offshore," replied Eggbert.

Awoo took a deep breath. "I'd better get on with it then, before the nerves get to me."

They went to the entrance of the cave and walked along the ledge behind the waterfall. Eggbert handed the painting brush to Zag, who pointed it at the sky. In a flash the hole in the cloud was filled and the sunlight blotted out. They watched Awoo fly into the darkness and out to sea, then went back into the cave to wait for his return.

Eraser and Artless had already clambered aboard the *Mobsea Dick*, accompanied by four Eradicators. Eraser pulled out a clothes brush to relieve his finery of anything that might have brushed against him as he boarded the rancid ship. "Maybe at last we are getting somewhere," he said to Artless, once more enjoying the darkness and preening himself.

"Uh . . . lamp der lights," ordered Catpone.

"Light the lamps . . . ya mean . . ." Gutrumble half-whispered.

"Uh . . . Guts, don't be nasty . . . I fink I'm quite genewous."

Eraser turned to Artless and sighed. "Give me strength."

"Where are the two brats?" asked Artless.

"Dere locked in da hold," said Spooky.

A small breeze made Eraser pause and sniff.

"FFWAAR, THIS HORRIBLE MOULDY HULK OF ROTTING WOOD STINKS!" he shouted, putting a pomander to his nose.

"It's dis weally fwendly atmosphere you've bwought wiv yuh," muttered Legs Diamonte sarcastically.

Eraser felt something wriggle in his frizzy mop of hair. "BUG SPRAY, SOMEBODY!" he shouted, vigorously waving his spindly hands.

An Eradicator produced a spray from under his black cloak. "Sar!"

"NOT NEAR MY NOSE!" Eraser's already horrible features contorted as he screwed up his face. "A. . .A. . .Atish . . .Attttisshshooooo!"

"Hey, Guts. He makes you look weally 'andsome," whispered Legs.

Eraser recovered. "You're pushing your luck . . . FLEA PIT."

Legs Diamonte was not happy. "Hey, Catpone, he called me a flea pit. What ya gonna do 'bout it?"

"UH . . .nuffink," said Catpone timidly.

"NUFFINK?" she screamed. "And I fought yaluved me."

"Uh . . . I do, I do," said Catpone meekly.

"WILL SOMEONE SHUT HER UP!" shouted Eraser impatiently.

"Why, you . . .YOU AWWOGANT, BOIL-WIDDEN BEANPOLE!" Legs rushed towards Eraser and, before anybody could stop her, she let fly a paw. Her long claws tore into Eraser's cheek.

"Uh. . .sh. . .she didn't mean it," shouted Catpone nervously.

Eraser was dumbfounded. The others stared in

amazement as an Eradicator gave him a handkerchief and Eraser dabbed quietly at his wound. He suddenly erupted. "SHE DIDN'T MEAN IT!" He looked at Artless. "Well, that's all right then . . . she didn't mean it."

Legs just studied her nails for damage, then looked defiantly at Eraser. "You weally do get wight up my nose."

"LOCK HER IN THE HOLD WITH THOSE TWO KIDS!" Eraser shouted. "Think of something horrible to teach her a lesson before you put her in Collage."

"Like stuffing stingy nettles up her nose," said Artless.

"Try a pineapple," said Eraser, still dabbing his face.

Legs held on firmly to her fake diamond-encrusted evening-bag as two Eradicators caught hold of her. "Call yourself Mogsters!" she shouted as she was taken down to the hold. "Yuh ALL WIMPS!"

Eraser was determined to get on with the nasty business at hand. "RIGHT, the rest of you FUR-BALLS, take me to those kids."

Awoo landed high up in the crow's-nest, in time to watch Eraser and his men cautiously follow Catpone and Gutrumble across the slippery, algae-ridden deck.

Awoo silently chuckled as he watched Eraser step on a particularly slimy part of the deck, then splat awkwardly on to the greasy filth.

"Careful as ya go," said Gutrumble with more than a hint of sarcasm, helping Eraser up and pretending to wipe the dirt off his clothes with an even dirtier handkerchief.

Eraser grabbed the trilby off Gutrumble's head, pushed him aside and trampled the hat into the slime. With great deliberation, he then placed the dripping trilby back on to Gutrumble's head, stretching it down over his gobsmacked eyes. "Listen, you slobbering over-sized bag of blubber, if this ship is not cleaned from top to bottom by the time we leave, I will PERSONALLY put you in Collage. GOT IT?"

Gutrumble's gross belly visibly gulped in fright. "S. . .s. . .SPOOKY!"

"Yeah, Guts." Spooky appeared from behind some rigging.

"You and da crew, clean up dis tub NOW!"

"Since when are ya giv'n der orders?" asked Spooky defiantly.

"Uh . . . we've enuff pwoblems . . . Do as he says . . . okay, Spooky? Uh . . . and quick, uh?"

Boiling with frustration, Eraser pointed his sneering, hooked nose at Catpone, peered through his cruel, narrow eyes and said, "For the VERY LAST TIME of asking, TAKE ME TO THOSE KIDS!"

Awoo heaved a sigh of relief, safe in the knowledge that all on board had been far too preoccupied to notice his arrival. He shuddered, realizing the really tricky bit of his task was yet to come. "How do I follow them without being seen?" he asked himself.

Lucy and William were as surprised as they were frightened when Legs Diamonte was thrown into the hold with them.

"Hi, cutie-pies," she said, rummaging in her evening-bag.

"What are you doing down here?" asked Lucy, plucking up courage and thinking how pretty Legs would really be if she wore less eyeshadow.

"Twouble wiv me is I can't keep my gob shut . . . I'm implosive," she sighed.

"Impulsive," William suggested politely.

"Dat's it, kid." Legs took out her powder compact. "Anyways, dat Ewaser weally gets wight up my pwitty little nose." She meticulously dabbed at her face, as the deck timbers above them creaked under the thudding boots of Eraser and his followers. "Didn't take dose wimps long," she said nonchalantly, as Lucy and William clung tightly to each other. "Don't say nuffink to 'em. Leave all da verbal to me."

Eraser hardly had time to peer into the hold before Legs greeted him and Catpone with a stream of seemingly endless abuse.

Aboard the Mobsea Dick

Awoo had no option but to patiently bide his time. The *Mobsea Dick* had become a hive of activity as the crew busily scrubbed the lantern-lit decks and hauled buckets over the side to fetch water from the sea. Awoo, spotting an untidy pile of canvas sails lying in a heap next to a half-open hatch, saw his opportunity. Hearing the ranting and raving coming from below decks, he was about to peep down the hatch, when a bucket clanked on the deck the other side of the mouldy pile of sails.

"Come on, ya lazy swabs, move dis heap," shouted Spooky.

Some of the crew members began cursing their way towards the mess. Awoo had to move quickly.

"Come on, stop complaining and get on wiv it, or I'll feed ya to der sharks," Spooky went on.

With no alternative, Awoo dived down into the hatch, just managing to control his landing and miss falling into the barrel of a cannon. Luckily it gave him something to hide behind as Eraser returned from the hold with his men, followed by Catpone and Gutrumble.

"I knew dose kids wud say nuffink," said Gutrumble.

"UH . . . dey couldn't get a word in, uh . . . sideways, wiv my poor Legs spouting off all der time," said Catpone.

"Edgeways, boss."

"Uh, yeah. It's dose brats' fault my twoo luv's dere in der last place."

"First place, boss," corrected Gutrumble.

"Uh? . . .Anyways, I oughta make 'em walk der uh . . . plonk."

"Plank, boss."

Catpone was wondering how he could rescue Legs. "Uh . . . plink . . . plonk . . . plunk . . . whatever, who cares?" he replied.

As Eraser stopped alongside the cannon and turned around to face Catpone and Gutrumble, his high-booted left foot just missed treading on Awoo's tail feathers. "Will you two morons SHUT UP!" he yelled, while picking at his nose. "Wait a minute!" he said gleefully. "That could be a good idea, making those horrible kids walk the plank."

"They can't talk if they're dead," said Artless.

"Good thinking," said Eraser. "We'll leave

them in the festering, rat-ridden hold of this floating bucket of garbage. That should loosen their wretched little tongues . . ."

"Uh . . . an' give 'em ear-ache," interrupted Catpone miserably.

". . . AND THEN, we'll drown them," said Eraser, with a sickly sneer.

Gutrumble decided to rest his heavily overburdened legs by sitting on the end of the cannon. As he sat down, his digestive system also took the cue to relax by letting off a series of muffled pops that sounded very similar to a sack-full of half-damp exploding bangers. Scared out of his wits, Awoo broke his cover.

The energy that erupted from Gutrumble at the sight of a potential meal on wings was extraordinary. Awoo first dodged Catpone, then the Eradicators, but Gutrumble whipped out a paw and with one swipe knocked the owl senseless.

Gutrumble picked Awoo up by his legs and dangled him first in front of the others, then close to his dribbling mouth. "Hello, dozy burdy. Bye-bye, rats," he burped.

"DON'T EVEN ATTEMPT IT," shouted Eraser. "Put the owl in the hold with the kids."

"Seems their friends are already coming to find them," said Artless.

"What ya talking about? Dis burdy lost its way. Tell 'em, boss," said Gutrumble, desperately wanting to enjoy a tasty snack.

"Artless, try explaining to these dim-wits."

"Owls don't normally fly out to sea in the dark, or at any other time. Therefore this one must have had a very special reason to come here. GET IT?"

"Wemember Legs is wiv 'em, said Gutrumble.

"Nah, she's stwictly, uh . . . vegaquarium," said Catpone, longing for a curvy, furry cuddle.

"Vegetarian, boss."

"Nah, stoopid . . . she likes fish," said Catpone.

Gutrumble unhitched a dead rat from his belt, nonchalantly stuffed all of it in his mouth, then spat out the tail.

"I hope for your sake that the deck is clean when I get up top, you greasy mess of fur," said Artless.

"Right, you!" said Eraser, choosing an Eradicator. "Make sure those idiots lock this owl in the hold with the brats and that mouthy . . ." he dabbed his sore cheek . . . "FELINE FLEA PIT."

"And stay on board and guard them until we send for you," Artless added as he, Eraser and the other Eradicators left to board the *Sea Err*.

The Eradicator took no notice of the twins' pleadings as he lifted the heavy wooden grid to the hold.

"Will you please let us out of here?" shouted Lucy.

"If you don't, you will be sorry. You'll see!" William shouted.

"Give me that owl, Gutrumble," the Eradicator ordered.

With great reluctance, Gutrumble passed him the dazed owl.

"WIMP!" shouted Legs Diamonte.

"A friend of yours, as if you didn't know," said the Eradicator, tossing Awoo into the hold.

Fortunately, he fell straight into Lucy's outstretched arms.

The hatch was shut and bolted, leaving Awoo, Legs and the twins imprisoned in semi-darkness . . .

Shafts of dim light from the lantern hanging above the grid roamed across the floor of the dank hold, swinging in harmony with the slight sway of the ship.

"Poor Awoo!" exclaimed Lucy, gently placing him on an old sail.

"Ya know dis burd, den?" said Legs, bending over Lucy's shoulder and taking a close look.

"You wouldn't, would you?" said Lucy, in a pleading tone of voice.

"I like fish if dat's whattya mean," said Legs, smiling.

William looked at the limp bird. "Do you think

he's dead?"

"Have they gone?" said Awoo, with one eye open, hoping he didn't need to play dead any longer. It was then that he saw the big white cat "Oh   my . . ." he gasped.

"Hello, sweety, or is it tweety?" Legs chuckled at her little joke. "Anyways, yuh okay cos I only like ostrich feathers."

"And f. . .fish," said Awoo, still taken aback. "What's she doing here?

"Not sure, but the rats have kept clear," said William informatively.

"My name's Legs Diamonte." Legs flashed her fake diamond necklace in the shafts of lantern light.

"But what's sh. . . uh, Legs doing here?" asked Awoo.

Legs sighed purrfully. "Dat's a stowy and a half, but basically my gob's gotta pwoblem."

Awoo looked blank and was about to ask what a "gob" was, when William spoke instead. "How did you get here, Awoo?"

"That would also take some explaining, old chap. Zag and Eggbert sent me to find you."

"We'll catch our death of cold if we stay here much longer," said Lucy, touching the wet timbers and listening to the sound of lapping water.

"Zag and Eggbert will be wondering what has

happened to me," said Awoo.

Zag and Eggbert had been waiting anxiously. Eggbert suddenly saw something in Zag's kindly face that he had not seen before. The mischievous laughing eyes were fixed and determined, and a strong, energetic, youthful glow shone radiantly through. Zag smiled confidently. "Let's show Eraser and his Eradicators what a Thingummagadgetician can really do."

Zag delicately negotiated the craft between the rock face and the waterfall. Almost immediately they were hovering under the gooey black cloud, looking down at the dark sea through the observation window.

Zag focused the telescope on the galleons. "First we watch and wait." He handed the brush to Eggbert. "If the Cameracraft spot us, bring back the daylight." He scanned the decks of the *Sea Err*, then said, "Mmm, how does Eraser blot out the sky?"

"Ya must have seen that for yarself when ya beamsurfed through the Galaxy of Ideas."

Zag thought about his spectacular journey. "The fiery comets, all colours of the rainbow, were the good ideas. They chased and crashed into huge, porridge-like blobs, the bad ideas, exploding them into a clouds of gooey mist."

"Absolutely right on the button," smiled

Eggbert. "But ya also must have seen that the blobs devoured more of the fiery comets."

"And they build up the thick, gooey black cloud over this island," said Zag thoughtfully, "blotting out creativity."

Eggbert nodded. "So ya see, Eraser upset the balance of things by stealing the Orb, and the bad ideas overwhelmed the good ideas."

Zag was conscious of Eggbert staring at him. "Is there a problem?"

Eggbert cleared his throat. "This is a bit embarrassing." His voice lowered to a husky whisper. "Ya see, it was my job to make sure the power of creativity stopped that happening."

"I can't think of any eagle who could do that." Zag smiled.

"That's the point. I'm Elan, the Spirit of Vigour. I balance power and strength," he said proudly. "Eggna is Vertu, the Spirit of Style. She turns the special into extra special. We're not just ordinary eagles, ya know."

"I know," Zag said.

"How do ya know?" said Eggbert.

"Well, for a start, there's nothing ordinary about this place," said Zag, passing the telescope to Eggbert. "Look, there's some big cats on that galleon having a party."

No Holes Barred

Legs Diamonte had hardly stopped talking since she had been thrown in the hold, and Lucy, William and Awoo were beginning to suffer from acute ear-bashing. Her droning on and on about how she was not putting up with Eraser, Catpone and the rest of the Mogsters left very little room to get a word in. She had nodded in sympathy at the sad plight of Flewy and Eggna, but this only happened when she was busy applying a different-coloured lipstick.

William had been fascinated by the prolific number of items Legs crammed into her small evening-bag. He had wondered if it could be thingummagadgetal like Zag's Thingummajacket. But there again, he'd noticed most ladies' handbags were the same, so he decided maybe it wasn't.

Legs was rambling on about how she longed for the blue skies to return, and how the weather, forever changing from cold and damp to clammy, did nothing at all for a girl's complexion, when an Eradicator shouted through the grid, "STOP THAT INCESSANT TALKING, YOU OLD BOOT!"

"SHUT YUR GOB, WALLYCATOR!" Legs yelled, enlightening Awoo as to the meaning of "gob".

"At least yours will be shut soon," called back the Eradicator, his high boots thudding overhead as he went above decks.

"We must get out of this mess," said Lucy.

"Dat's what I've been saying," said Legs, about to carry on where she had left off.

"We must think and talk positively!" said Awoo, staring pointedly at Legs.

Lucy pulled up the right leg of her track-suit, reached into her long sock and brought out the painting brush. "I managed to hide this."

"Oooh, dat looks pwitty," said Legs. "What is it?"

"Sort of like a wand," said Lucy.

"Wha' . . . like weal magic?"

Lucy smiled. "No, it is better than magic . . . it's thingummagadgetal."

"Trouble is, we don't know how to use it properly," said William. "We nearly landed in the sea when we came here."

"We have been afraid to use it in case we made a mistake and took the cats . . . um, no offence, Legs

. . . and the ship back home with us," added Lucy.

"No good if ya can't use it, dat's what I always say," said Legs, studying her nails.

"Remember Flewy's lavatree?" said William.

"Don't wemind me of toilets," said Legs, crossing her legs.

"Who could forget?" Lucy chuckled. "All Zag asked him to do was think of a tree."

"We could concentrate on what we want the brush to do," said William.

"Let's do it while there's nobody about," said Lucy.

"Do what? That is the first thing we need to decide," said Awoo.

"Escape of course," said William impatiently.

"We need to plan properly, not just try any-thing," said Lucy.

"Exactly," agreed Awoo.

"Then what about painting a hole in the grid that's big enough for us to climb through?" suggested William.

"We need a rope to be able to climb out," said Lucy.

"Dat's okay. I could jump up and get one," said Legs, nonchalantly putting away her nail file.

"You mean you'll help us?" Awoo asked.

"Listen, tweety-pie, ya don't sewiously fink I'm

gonna stay in dis mess for der west of my life, do ya?"

"I . . . uh, suppose not . . . and . . . uh, thank you," said Awoo, as much surprised as he was grateful.

"When a gal's made up 'er mind . . . den she's made up 'er mind . . . if ya know what I mean." Legs purposefully tidied the items in her evening-bag. "I ain't putting up wiv it no more, and anuvver fing, fwom now on Catp . . ."

"Looks like you've made up your mind then," William interrupted, hoping to stop her in mid-flow. ". . .Catpone will 'ave to wun after me for a change."

"Good, that's settled," said Awoo, desperately trying to stop her mouth from running a full marathon.

"William, Legs and I could try to climb up to the crow's-nest," Lucy suggested. "Hopefully they won't think to look for us there."

"Nah, dat's no good," said Legs.

"Then what do you suggest?" asked William.

"Simple. We'll climb down a wope, nick der dinghy and escape to der beach."

"Sounds good," said Lucy.

"I will escape out of one of the open gun ports and fetch Eggbert and Zag," said Awoo.

The plan was coming together. There were some loose ends, but at least it was a plan.

"Let's do it den," said Legs, tying her evening-bag to her belt.

"I hope Eggbert is still waiting for me," said Awoo.

Lucy pointed the brush at the heavy wooden grid and closed her eyes in deep concentration. A large hole appeared in the centre of the grid, and Awoo flew through it and perched on a nearby cannon.

Legs showed off her agility by springing out of the hold in one mighty leap. As quietly as possible she quickly found a long piece of rope and dragged it towards the grid. From above came the sound of raucous laughter and shouting. The crew seemed to be well into their rum-filled mugs.

"Wimps, der lot of 'em!" said Legs, quickly dropping one end of the rope either side of a remaining grid spar, allowing it to be secured by the twins. "Huwwy up, will yuh?" she urged.

William climbed up first, then lent a hand to Lucy as she clambered through the hole. Lucy slipped the painting brush back into her sock, and they swiftly followed Legs to the port side of the galleon.

Crouched on the ledge of a gun port, Legs precariously stretched out to reach the rope ladder that hung down to the dinghy. Pulling it towards her and gripping it firmly, she helped the twins to climb on to it.

"Hold tight, kids, cos as I get on, it ain't half gonna sway a bit."

Awoo perched on a protruding rusty cannon and watched to make sure all was well before he flew off. "Take care," he whispered to them. "I will return with Zag and Eggbert as soon as possible."

All hell broke loose on the *Mobsea Dick* as the Eradicator stormed up to the top deck after a routine check on his prisoners.

"THEY'VE ESCAPED . . . YOU IDIOTS!"

"Uh . . . WHAT!" Catpone panicked, running around in circles. "Find 'em, ya lazy swabs, uh . . . uvarwise we're in weal twouble."

Spooky looked over the port side. "Hey, boss, dere in der wowing boat." He took a longer look, his feline eyes penetrating the darkness. "And it looks like yuh Legs 'as gone."

"Uh . . . dey look okay to me," said Catpone, looking at his boots.

"Nah, boss, I mean da dinghy . . . Look!"

Catpone did, couldn't believe it, looked again and immediately became distraught. "Uh . . . my Legs 'as gone!" he yelled.

Gutrumble wandered over, burped and put a large, grotty paw on his boss's shoulder. "Must be all dat wum we dwank."

"LOWER THE OTHER DINGHY, YOU BUFFOONS!" ordered the Eradicator.

"UH . . . yeah, w. . .we'll go after dem," said Catpone.

"NO, YOU WON'T!" barked the Eradicator. "I'm using that to take me to the *Sea Err*. I am reporting your stupidity to Eraser. YOU'RE ALL IN BIG TROUBLE!"

Gutrumble swung a hefty paw, which pole-axed the Eradicator. "My boss has lost his twoo luv, so we're taking der dinghy and dat's dat," he said, picking up the unfortunate heap and throwing him over the side of the *Mobsea Dick*.

"Now we're in weal twouble," said Spooky, launching the dinghy.

Gutrumble held on to the rope. "If yuh soaking wet, ya can't get any wetter," he said profoundly.

With a big splash, the dinghy dropped into the water.

"Uh . . . well, I'm dwy," said Catpone, having jumped into it.

"If it wained bwains, yuh wouldn't get wet, boss," said Spooky.

"Uh . . . dat's okay den," said Catpone some-what confused, as they rowed feverishly after the twins and Legs.

Legs had never rowed a boat before. Under the simple instruction to "keep it straight", she had taken the tiller, while William and Lucy rowed hard towards the beach. The in-coming tide brought luck with its flow, greatly aiding their progress.

"I wish Zag would hurry up," puffed William.

Legs pointed to the cloud. "Is dat 'im?" she asked. "Maybe it's a marriage?"

"Mirage," said William, as the dinghy temporarily lost its direction, then grounded itself on the sandy beach.

Lucy and William had no chance to confirm one way or the other. The shouting from the Mogsters' boat could be heard clearly, and was far too close for comfort.

They jumped into the shallow water and raced on to the beach. Lucy looked back, then reached for the painting brush. "We must divert their attention, so we have time to hide." She pointed the brush at the chasing dinghy and within a flash it shone luminous pink. Taken by complete surprise, the Mogsters stopped rowing.

"Vewy pwitty," said Legs, as they rushed into the cover of the dense, withered palm trees. "Dat fingymawicket yuh got is clever, ain't it?"

The Battle in the Sky

The luminous-pink dinghy caught Zag's attention. "It's about time we switched the lights on," he said, steadying the Beamsurfer. Eggbert slid open the door and drew a large hole in the cloud, and the sunlight blazed through once more.

"Now don't they just look dandy in pink?" Eggbert said with a chuckle.

Zag had spotted Awoo flying low towards the cliffs. "We'll get Awoo first, then deal with them," they announced.

The Beamsurfer zoomed across to Awoo. Zag kept it hovering a short but safe distance from him, and he gratefully flew aboard.

"Thank heavens you're safe," said Zag. "We missed you."

"Ya okay, pal?" said Eggbert happily, sliding the door shut.

Awoo took a gulp of air. "Am I glad to see both

you chaps." Then without further ado he briefed them on Flewy's capture and how Legs Diamonte had helped him and the twins escape.

Zag wasted no time in swooping down on the Mogsters. They gasped when the Beamsurfer appeared as if from nowhere and hovered over their bizarre dinghy. The Beamsurfer's door slid open.

"Where are the children?" Zag shouted.

"Uh . . . I . . . I want my Legs back, dat's all," shouted Catpone. "Uh . . . dey wen off to der woods."

Watching from the poop-deck, Eraser focused his telescope on the Beamsurfer and the pink dinghy. A sickly, sneering grin slid across his face. "Well, well, what a pretty sight," he said, handing the telescope to Artless.

Artless adjusted the focus. "Looks like we have them in our grasp."

"Send your men to capture that craft and wipe out ALL the rest, including the brats in the woods," barked Eraser. "Then go and transfer that seagull and eagle into Collage and wait there for me."

"Does all include Catpone and his Mogsters?" queried Artless.

"YES! ALL includes those filthy, smelly cats and their grotty ship."

The sky roared with the sound of five

Cameracraft, speeding in formation towards the Beamsurfer.

Lucy, William and Legs watched the impending mayhem from comparative safety behind some fallen palm trees.

"I fink yuh fwend has his work cut up," said Legs.

"Cut out," said Lucy, watching intently.

"Collage is near here," said Legs, in a matter-of -fact sort of way.

"Do you know how to get there?" asked William.

"Finking of wescuing yuh pals, are ya?" Legs asked.

"We are staying right here and waiting for Zag," said Lucy firmly.

"Seems like ya may 'ave some waiting to do," said Legs, watching the Beamsurfer zoom high into the sky to do battle with the Cameracraft.

"I thought that once you were in Collage there was no escape," said Lucy.

"I'm pwitty sure dey 'aven't been back to Collage since dey captured Flewy. So yuh pal may be stuck in a prismatran waiting to be twansferred."

"If there's a chance, we've got to try," said William with conviction. "It may be too late if we wait for Zag."

"Prismatran?" asked Lucy.

"I'll tell ya as we go," said Legs.

Afloat in their dinghy the three Mogsters took full advantage of their grandstand position. "Looks like deyre goners, boss," said Spooky.

"Uh . . . don't count ya itchings before they scratch," said Catpone, seeing one of the Cameracraft veer off in their direction.

"Chickens before they . . . never mind, boss," groaned Gutrumble.

"Whatever," said Catpone, not averting his gaze for a moment.

"I fink it's coming to get us, boss," said Spooky, immediately diving into the sea to take cover under their boat. Without hesitation, Catpone and Gutrumble followed Spooky's cue.

Thinking that the Mogsters had fled the boat, the Eradicator swooped his craft away from the dinghy and made his return to the battle in the sky.

Zag put the Beamsurfer into a loop-the-loop, then slowed down, allowing a Cameracraft to get right on his tail.

"It's going shoot us!" said Awoo, totally amazed at Zag's actions.

Zag smiled. "Exactly. Trust me!"

A brilliant flash from the Cameracraft engulfed

the Beamsurfer. Zag pulled blindly at the joystick and the Beamsurfer did another big loop.

As Eggbert's eyes recovered, he could see that four out of the five Cameracraft were left. "Amazing! I thought that dude had got us fair and square!"

"The surface of the Beamsurfer reflected the image back to the Cameracraft," said Zag with a huge grin.

"Ya mean it captured itself?" said Eggbert.

"That's exactly what I mean," said Zag, smiling.

Two Cameracraft bombarded the Beamsurfer with a deluge of blinding flashes. Zag pulled the joystick, taking the Beamsurfer on a steep upward climb. He levelled the craft and turned it back towards the sea.

"One more to go," said Eggbert, scanning the sky.

"Look," said Zag, "it's coming out of the sunlight."

"And it's heading straight for us," said Awoo frantically.

Zag tried desperately to put the Beamsurfer on evasion course, but it was too late. They braced themselves for a head-on collision, but the Cameracraft disappeared into thin air in another blinding flash.

For a brief moment a sixth Cameracraft hovered alongside the Beamsurfer. Its pilot waved a black-gloved hand before the Cameracraft suddenly veered away and headed towards the peninsula.

"What the. . .?" Eggbert was near dumbstruck. "It saved us."

Zag flew the Beamsurfer back to the Mogsters and hovered close above their dinghy. Gutrumble was struggling to get his bulk back on board, aided by Catpone and Spooky, who were trying with great difficulty to haul in their sodden friend.

"Oh dear, he nearly made it then," said Awoo sarcastically.

Zag opened the door of the Beamsurfer. "So much for Eraser helping his men," he called out, drawing   attention to the fact that the *Sea Err* had hoisted its sails and was heading towards the peninsula.

"Why hasn't Legs come out from hiding?" asked Eggbert, expecting to have seen her and the twins on the beach by the edge of the sea.

"Cos she's left der boss," puffed Spooky, finally pulling Gutrumble by the seat of his over-burdened pants back into the dinghy.

"Uh . . . says she's 'ad enuff," said Catpone, "and now she's bweedy."

"Broody?" Zag queried.

"Uh . . . yuh, dat's it. Uh . . . if der twuth be

known, we've all 'ad enuff," said Catpone wearily.

"She's gone so daft, I woodunt put it past her tuh be showing dem kids awound Collage," said Spooky.

"Uh . . . yeah. Uh . . . we've all been vewy fwightened dat Ewaser wud educate us by sending us tuh . . . College," said Catpone.

"He means ewadicate us and send us to Collage. No one's never learned him how to talk proper like me," said Gutrumble apologetically.

Zag looked very serious. "Do you know the inside of Collage?"

"Uh . . . yah kidding? Ewaser evun gave me uh picture of it to wemind me dat I don't wanna go dere. It's 'anging in my, uh . . . cabinet.""

"Cabin, boss," Gutrumble corrected.

"Yeah, we looks at it evewy day weligiously. It makes us stick to Ewaser's wules," said Spooky.

The Beamsurfer made a swishy, whirry sound as Zag manoeuvred it next to the dinghy and locked it in positional mode.

"Uh . . . what'ya doing?" shouted Catpone. "Uh . . . uh, please . . . uh, 'onest, we don't want twouble no more, anyhow."

"I'm giving you a chance to help us," said Zag, stepping into the stern of the dinghy. The Mogsters looked on with apprehensive curiosity as he rummaged in his Thingummajacket and pulled out a hairspray-sized aerosol with a built-in telescopic aerial. "I need your picture. Then, with luck, we'll find the children and Legs," said Zag. He fixed the aerosol on the transom with two and a half spots of Thingummagadgetal Magnafix – a magnetic glue so powerful it could even magnetize wood.

"Uh . . .what's dat exactly?" asked Catpone, rather bemused.

"My Jettican," said Zag, pulling out the aerial. "It's a powerful ozone-friendly aerosol mini-jet engine."

The Mogsters' befuddled faces told Zag that action was the best description. "Just sit down and hold on tight," he said, stepping back into the Beamsurfer.

Zag looked at the amazed Eggbert and Awoo. "We're taking them to the *Mobsea Dick* to get the picture of Collage." He reached into his Thingummajacket, then handed a small remote-control device to Eggbert. "Red button to start or stop, the lever is for forward, reverse, left and right. But be careful, that boat will go like a rocket!"

"Sit tight, ya guys," shouted Eggbert, eager to give the Mogsters the fright of their lives as he put Zag's device through its paces. "See ya by the *Mobsea Dick*." He winked at Awoo. "Or maybe just past it."

Inside Horrible Collage

Strewn like soldiers long since fallen in battle, trees lay silent and tangled in their sad decay. The steep path wound its lonely upward journey to the mouth of the volcano. Pausing for rest, Lucy, William and Legs looked down at the dreary, desolate landscape now steaming in the heat of the glorious sunshine. The whole putrid scene bore stark witness to the evil doings of Eraser. Noticing derelict hamlets scattered around and about, William asked who had lived there.

"Dat's der villages where der Wutilans lived," said Legs.

Lucy was not sure whether she had heard correctly. "Wutilans?"

"Nah, Wutilans," said Legs.

"Rutilans?" said William.

"Dat's wight, Wutilans."

"What did they do?" asked Lucy.

"Dere job was putting der glow in der sunset . . . " Legs paused and smiled longingly. "Ah, ya should 'ave seen dere glowing 'appy little faces. Dat's until Ewaser blotted out der sunset an' put dem all in Collage!"

"So why did you Mogsters help Eraser?" asked William boldly.

"We fought it wus bowing bein' all nice wiv evwyfing all jus' so and dat, an' cos Ewaser offud us exiting fings."

"This is all so sad," said Lucy, looking around at the lifeless island.

"We all make mistakes, and dat was a biggun. Anyways, now we're going to put it wight wiv der help of yuh fingymawicket."

"And Zag," said William.

"Especially Zag," agreed Lucy.

"We can't stop here. We need to climb up to der top of dis old volcano."

William looked up at the daunting prospect. "That'll take ages."

"We gotta do it, cos it's hollow and Collage is inside it."

"Then let's paint a tunnel into it," said William, proud of his suggestion.

"Good idea," agreed Lucy, taking the painting brush from out of her long sock.

The sunlight didn't penetrate very far into the tunnel, so they relied on Legs's keen eyesight to see them through. Fortunately, Lucy had thought of a nice smooth, straight tunnel, so it was easy under foot. It was not long before they could see the big shaft of sunlight shining through the huge hole at the top of the old volcano.

"Dere's Collage. It looks exactly like der picture in Catpone's cabin," whispered Legs.

The twins gasped as they stared at the huge, flat, rocky wall opposite them. At first sight it seemed like a jumble of graffiti. But as they looked harder, they could make out very sad-looking, flattened images randomly mixed underneath and on top of each other. Cautiously peering over the edge, they discovered their tunnel brought them out at least ten yards above the vast cavern floor that shelved into a subterranean lagoon.

The sheer Collage rock wall rose over half-way up towards the mouth of the volcano.

"Wow! That must be the size of a football pitch," whispered William in wonder.

"Are all those images from Blot?" Lucy asked.

"Nah, I fink Ewaser's got images fwom lots of uvver places." Legs looked up, down and around. "Dis is too 'igh up fuh me tuh jump down and dere's nowhere to put my paws."

"Then we'll draw some steps," said Lucy. She pulled the painting brush from out of her sock and was about to draw steps when below them a tall figure dressed in black entered the cavern.

"Dat's Artless the Heartless," said Legs.

Transfixed, they watched silently as a huge solid stone plinth, big enough to park at least four cars and a few bicycles on, ground its way up from the cavern floor. Artless took two prismatrans from his cloak. Placing them apart on the plinth, he stood back. Bars made of purple light beamed up from the four edges forming a tall cage. The prismatrans glowed white, releasing their captives into the cage of purple light.

"NOT ANOTHER BIG FLIPPING EAGLE!" screeched a familiar voice. "AND THIS ONE'S GOT A FLASHING GREEN FOOT!"

Lucy gasped, not believing their luck. "There's Flewy and Eggna."

"See, told ya dey might not 'ave bin twans-ferred yet," said Legs.

"Who are you?" said Eggna, looking down at her loud-beaked companion.

"I'm Flewy. I know who you are, and that bloke out there must be Smarty Arty."

"There is no time for this, Eggna," said Artless. "You must give me the Stone of Imagination."

"What, after you betrayed me and my mate?" said Eggna, clutching the brilliant green stone tightly in her talon. "No chance!"

"I have little time. I will take it off you, if I have to," said Artless.

"I'd like to see you try," Eggna said confidently.

"Yeah, you tell him," said Flewy, shadow-boxing. "I'll back you up."

Legs could see that the height and size of the cage made it just possible for her to jump down on to. She figured that if the cage could hold the birds in, then it could hold her out. With a mighty leap, she sprang from the edge of the tunnel on to the top of the cage. Her paws missed the bars and she fell to the floor, knocking herself unconscious.

"WAAAAAAARK! CAAAATS!" shrieked Flewy, crashing into Eggna in an attempt to take cover behind her. The jolt made Eggna lose grip of the stone and it rolled out of the cage in front of Artless's feet.

Lucy and William watched in horror as Artless captured Legs with his flashgun, then ejected the prismatran from its handle. He stood back from the cage of purple light and, as it disappeared into the stone plinth, he returned Flewy and Eggna to their prismatrans. Artless pressed a button at the side of the plinth and a projector appeared from out of its surface. He placed the three prismatrans in the projector and shone them on the Collage wall, making sure each image was plain to see.

"We can't just do nothing," said Lucy. She pointed the brush down the wall and in a flash stone steps appeared. "Don't do this," she cried out as she and William rushed down into the cavern.

But it was too late. Artless had made the transfer to Collage. Lucy ran to the awful wall and stood sobbing in front of the motionless images of Flewy, Legs and Eggna.

"You're nothing but a BIG, NASTY, HORRIBLE BULLY!" shouted William helplessly, putting his arm around his sister.

"This is not what it may seem," Artless called out, staring at them from across the cavern. He started to reach inside his cloak, and the twins backed up against the Collage wall.

"NO! NO! PLEASE DON'T!" shouted William.

Panicking in her desire to escape, Lucy recklessly drew a magic circle. But the brush touched the collage and whisked them into the horrible picture in an unstoppable whirlwind of light.

They looked out and saw Artless staring at them. He shouted something, but they could not hear him. William put his hands up as if pressing against a thick sound-proofed glass window and shouted back. Artless stared for a moment longer, then ran out of the cavern.

"This is so weird," said William, pressing hard against the invisible barrier. "I can't feel anything, yet I can't push through it."

Lucy looked at the painting brush in her hand, decided crying was not the answer and said, "Easy, I'll paint a hole with the brush." A flash of light shot out from the brush but no hole appeared. She tried again and again until William stopped her.

"It's no use, Lucy. How can the brush paint on nothing?"

"Maybe there's another way out," Lucy said, trying hard to be optimistic.

They turned around and walked into the misty, flat images. There were so many of them stuck on top and underneath each other, that the further Lucy and William went in, the more murky it became, until they could hardly see each other.

"I'm frightened," said Lucy, squeezing William's hand. "This feels like a ghosts' graveyard."

William shuddered at the thought. "If we go any deeper, we will never find our way back to the light."

The Changing Sea Err

"I'm surrounded by fools!" Eraser cursed, climbing up
to the quarter-deck and walking towards the ship's
wheel. The sound of Artless's Cameracraft had
disturbed his train of thought. Up to that moment, he
had been in his cabin, curtains drawn, cursing the
sunlight and considering his next move. "Steady to
starboard, you IDIOT, we don't want to end up on
the reef."

The *Sea Err* sailed slowly between the sunlit
volcanic mountains that heralded the entrance to the
lagoon. Unused to daylight sailing, the crew were no
longer familiar with this final stretch of the journey.

"Lower the mainsail," ordered Eraser. "Jump to
it!" He leaned over the rail. Some of the crew on the
quarter-deck below were daydreaming. "QUICKER
THAN THAT!" he bawled.

The galleon pointed into the wind and the large
black sails fluttered obstinately as the crew set about
furling them neatly to the spars.

"Anchors aweigh," shouted Eraser.

The command echoed to the ship's bow via a few voices, and the anchors were dropped into the sea.

The dark cloud that had once cloaked the island was fast disappearing, leaving behind a blue sky, radiant with sunshine. A rainbow appeared against the remaining backdrop of gooey cloud, splashing into the sea and spraying its range of beautiful colours.

"What's going on?" asked an Eradicator.

"Creativity, you idiot. That's what's going on!" barked Eraser.

A silvery mist closed in and rolled across the sea towards the lagoon, engulfing the *Sea Err*. Sparkling raindrops poured down all around them, fizzing with colours as they hit every surface.

Eraser furiously brushed the rain-sparkles off his clothes with his hands. "This stuff had better not leave stains," he shouted.

The mist cleared as quickly as it had arrived. In its passing, the island had become lush and green again, and the air smelt pure.

A look of grim determination clouded the frenzied features of Eraser's face. Stamping the deck, he shouted at one of the crew, "Don't just stand there gawking!"

The crew member was secretly admiring the

beauty of the island. He could hardly remember the invigorating feeling of the rain-sparkles as they danced on his cheeks, but, like the rest of the crew, he was helpless against the evil of Eraser the Terrible.

"DISENGAGE THE FLIGHT DECK AND PREPARE TO RETRACT MASTS!" shouted Eraser impatiently.

The *Sea Err* lurched a little as the Cameracraft carrier parted company from the starboard side of the main ship, leaving the flight-deck crew to drop anchor from the stern of their section.

Eraser went below to his cabin and sat at his desk. He reached for his quill pen and pulled on it. The wood panelling in front of him opened, revealing a large screen. He twisted the pen and the surface of the desk parted, giving him access to a control panel. At the press of a button, each of the ship's masts retracted like a folding telescope. Then the furled sails folded umbrella-like, as each section of the mast closed into itself. He pressed another button and a transparent canopy the full length of the hull rose out of both sides of the ship, meeting in the middle and making a watertight cover over the whole of the ship. Like a caterpillar changing into a chrysalis, an amazing metamorphosis had taken place. The *Sea Err* had become a submarine. Through the Tannoy he shouted, "PREPARE TO DIVE."

The crew watched the water rise over the glass-like canopy as the *Sea Err* sank slowly into the wonder world. They looked agog at the sunlit beauty of the clear ocean. The downpour of sparkling rain had revived the sea and was already re-creating life on the once-dying coral reef.

Eraser became more and more concerned as he watched the crew sampling the long-forgotten wonders of creation. To his horror, they were obviously enthralled.

He piloted the *Sea Err* into the mouth of a huge underwater cavern that penetrated deep into the reef and led into the heart of the volcanic mountain. He watched the screen closely as they reached the open water of the subterranean lagoon of Collage. With one press of a button, the *Sea Err* surfaced in Collage and the canopy opened.

Eraser rushed down to the disembarkation port, ranting and raving. "Out of my way, scum!" he cried.

In his hurry to inspect the Collage wall, he nearly lost his footing as he climbed down the galleon's side steps on to the cavern floor.

"QUIET! LOOK HERE!" he shouted to the Eradicators, pointing out Flewy, Eggna and Legs. "Take this as an example to you ALL. No doubt Artless will soon return, having captured that inferior craft and its meddling occupants."

The crew got back to work, while Eraser gazed with partial satisfaction at the Collage wall and twiddled the brilliant white Stone of Genius hanging around his neck. Suddenly something caught his eye. Thinking he'd seen a movement, Eraser scrutinized the images of Flewy, Eggna and Legs. All was flat and motionless, so he dismissed the matter from his evil mind. Rubbing his spindly hands together with glee, he thought that Artless was probably at that very moment sinking the *Mobsea Dick*.

The final Chance

The mooring ropes attached to the Beamsurfer hummed a tune as they strained to rid themselves of the festering galleon. The glorious, sunny blue sky made the top deck of the *Mobsea Dick* a more acceptable place to be, although, from choice, it would still have been last on their list.

Zag had decided to create a team spirit from the outset of this unlikely relationship. "If Catpone agrees, the *Mobsea Dick* is our base for the time being."

"Uh . . . no pwoblem," agreed Catpone, "pwovided dat if ya stick dat Jetti . . . uh . . . fingy can on, ya don't give Eggbert der contwols."

The Mogsters had decided, after their involuntary wave-skimming ordeal, speed-boat racing was not for them – sailing was a far more sedate pastime.

Not all was in harmony on the top deck. Awoo was not at all happy to be in the company of the Mogsters and their crew, and it showed.

"Uh . . . look, we're weally, weally sowwy fa bein' nasty," said Catpone.

"Yeah, weally, weally," said Spooky, trying to make amends.

"Me! I know ya now. I luv ya! How could I eat ya? I even wanna kiss ya!" said Gutrumble, trying to look angelic.

For a moment Awoo looked decidedly ill.

"Yud betta pwomise ya won't kiss 'im," said Spooky.

"Look, I pwomise, cos we don't wanna live wiv Ewaser in der dark no more," said Gutrumble.

"Uh . . . and I want my Legs back," said Catpone.

Awoo relented. "This ship needs to be cleaned up."

"Hey, we 'ave cleaned it," said Spooky.

"Properly, old chap," said Awoo.

Zag wanted to avert the possible discord in this fragile partnership and concentrate on his plan. "First I need to have the picture of Collage."

"Uh . . . hey, Spooks, get der picture fwom my cabinet . . . I mean, cabin," said Catpone.

"I knows where ya mean, boss," said Spooky, grinning.

"See, evewybody's bein' 'elpful," said Gutrumble, for Awoo's benefit.

Awoo anxiously pointed to the Cameracraft gliding towards them from out of the sunshine. "This isn't helpful."

"Uh . . .t. . .take cover!" shouted Catpone.

"It's not going to attack us," said Zag calmly, having expected the return of the Cameracraft that saved them from the collision in the sky.

"Hey, what's dat cweep doing?" said Spooky, returning with the picture of Collage, as the Cameracraft hovered and settled down on the sea alongside the *Mobsea Dick*.

"We're about to find out," said Eggbert, going with Zag to the starboard side.

The canopy hissed open and a tall figure dressed in black stood out on his craft.

"You must be Astral," Zag called out.

"Artless the Heartless traitor, you mean!" shouted Eggbert angrily.

Zag interrupted. "Why are you here?"

"Because I am not a traitor and together we have this final chance to reunite the Orb of Brilliance before disaster befalls us all," came the direct reply. "You must allow me aboard."

Eggbert looked disbelievingly at Zag. "You can't! Not after all he's done!"

"We must. It could well be our last chance," said Zag firmly.

"But . . . ya . . ." Eggbert was dumbstruck, and so were all the others.

"Come aboard," shouted Zag. "The crew will help you." Once again, Zag spoke firmly to Eggbert. "Don't do anything stupid, even if Astral has the Stone of Imagination with him."

"If he has, I'll take it off him . . . like he did to Eggna."

"If you do, none of us may survive to regret that. You must keep control of your emotions." He touched Eggbert's wing. "Believe me and trust my judgement."

Eggbert thought, then smiled. "Okay, have no worries, my good friend. I've had faith in ya since we first met."

The tall, blond figure of Astral climbed aboard and made a friendly low salute to Eggbert, but the gesture was ignored.

Astral offered his hand to Zag. "You must be Zagwitz the Thingummagadgetician."

"I am." Zag shook his hand. "How do you know my name?"

"How could the Galaxy of Ideas and World of Creativity not be aware of your skills?" Astral smiled.

Zag thought the name Artless the Heartless seemed inappropriate for someone whose blue eyes and features looked so warm and friendly; the name Astral suited him much better. "Does Eraser know of me?"

"Normally he's too fond of himself to be aware of anyone else. But he is very bothered that you have the Orb and two stones," replied Astral.

"As I thought, Eraser has the other two stones now," said Eggbert.

"If you are referring to the Stone of Imagination," Astral delved into his cloak, "here it is."

Eggbert looked at the brilliant, shining green stone. He could feel his emotions rise and wanted to snatch it away, but Astral surprised him.

"You see, Eggbert, I trust you. Here, hold it. Now you have three stones to fit in the Orb."

Eggbert couldn't believe it. "Is this some kind of trick?" he said, handing the stone to Zag.

Zag brought out the Orb from his Thingummajacket. "It would be far too silly, if that were a trick," he said, locking the three stones together. Immediately the brilliance of the stones was boosted so much, he had no alternative but to shut the Orb.

"Astral, answer me this," said Eggbert. "Why did ya shoot Eggna?"

"Eraser saw you and Eggna carry away the stones from the deck of the *Sea Err.* He ordered the Cameracraft to shoot you. I had no option but to preserve my cover and hope at some time I could reverse the process."

Zag lifted his fez and scratched his head. "Eggbert, just think instead of letting your emotions run wild. If Astral was going to betray you, he would have had you captured as you swooped in, not after you had taken off with the stones."

Eggbert murmered, almost to himself, "And all along I thought ya'd used the stones as bait to catch us."

He looked decidedly ashamed of himself. He raised his wing in a friendly half-salute. "I am really sorry."

Astral gladly acknowledged the gesture.

"Well done," said Zag. "Seems we're all on the same side."

Suddenly there was a lot of shouting and commotion, as most of the crew ran towards the side of the ship and looked overboard.

"Boss! BOSS!" shouted Gutrumble. "Dat Ewadicator I fumped an' chucked overboard is nicking Artless's . . . I mean . . . Astwal's Camewacwaft!"

Catpone screamed at the Eradicator, "HEY. . . YA PINK!"

"Uh, he's a punk," corrected Gutrumble. "We're still pink."

Astral, Zag and Eggbert rushed to the ship's rails, but it was too late. The craft's canopy had closed and they watched helplessly as it took off.

"He's going to warn Eraser. We must move quickly," urged Astral.

Zag reached deep into his Thingummajacket and pulled out four Jetticans, a control device and four sticks of Magnafix.

"Eggbert will glue the Jetticans to the ship with the Magnafix, then explain to Spooky how to operate this control device," said Zag. "Astral and Eggbert will come with me on the Beamsurfer."

"What about me?" asked Awoo.

Astral pulled Zag aside. "I'm sure you have considered the Cameracraft may come back for the *Mobsea Dick*," he mentioned politely.

"BUT what about me?" Awoo asked again.

"Actually, Astral, I have an idea," said Zag, taking the painting brush and pointing it at the deck of the *Mobsea Dick*.

"BUT WHAT ABOUT M. . .?"

In a flash the galleon became shining silver. "That should help," said Zag, pleased with himself.

"Grab yuh shades an' giv' a pair to Awoo," Gutrumble shouted to the crew. "I fink he may be staying on board wiv us."

Awoo looked unsure as Zag whispered to him discreetly, "I'm not too confident about the Mogsters' navigational skills and their ability to get to Collage."

"How do I know how to get there?" asked Awoo.

Zag called Astral over. "Astral, could you help Awoo for a second?"

Eggbert flew back on deck. "The Jetticans are fixed in place."

Zag, Eggbert and Astral climbed aboard the Beamsurfer.

"Eraser's in for a big surprise," said Zag, placing Catpone's picture of Collage under the Beamsurfer's scanner.

A Beam Too Far

Eraser paced up, down and around the cavern with an ungainly gait that echoed his impatience for Artless's return. Thoughts crowded his warped mind; an endless list of nasty, evil things he was going to do to every planet, in every galaxy and indeed anywhere else he could find. He felt sure there was something different about Collage, but he couldn't figure out what had changed.

"I just saw something move in the wall," shouted an Eradicator, prompting the others to come and have a look.

"William, keep still," Lucy whispered. "More of the Eradicators are coming over to look."

"What are you whispering for? They can't hear us," said William.

Eraser rushed back over to the wall. "FOOL! WHERE? I CAN'T SEE ANYTHING MOVING IN THERE!" he shouted, trying hard to peer inside. To get closer, he bent double and bumped the oozy boil on his nose against the wall, making it very angry and him exceedingly so. "OOOOOOUCH! YOU IDIOTS!" he bawled painfully.

The soundless contortions displayed by Eraser hopping up and down were so hilarious that William forgot his dire situation. Jumping up, he pointed at Eraser. "Hahahahaha . . . look at him!"

Lucy tried to pull him back, but they had already been seen.

"Where's Artless? They're supposed to be flat and meaningless," Eraser roared, "not able to jump up and down!"

The twins discovered very quickly that, while they could not get out of Collage, neither could Eraser get in. Dodging about, they annoyed Eraser with their own version of cat and mouse, repeatedly thumbing their noses at him, then disappearing.

"We can't do this for ever," said Lucy after a while, feeling exhausted.

"One more time to make him bang his boil," cried William.

At that moment, Eraser's attention was drawn towards a soaking-wet Eradicator pushing his way through the other Eradicators.

"Out of my way! I must speak to Eraser!" shouted Soaking Wet.

"And where have you sprung from?" asked Eraser.

Soaking Wet splashed a salute. "The *Mobsea Dick*, Sar."

"DON'T DRIP ALL OVER ME!" Eraser roared. "DID YOU SWIM HERE OR WHAT?"

"I crashed by the reef, Sar."

"You crashed!" Eraser turned and looked at the others. "Hear that? He crashed by the reef. IN WHAT DID YOU CRASH, IMBECILE?"

Soaking Wet became very nervous. "The C. . .Cameracraft, Sar."

Eraser noticed that Soaking Wet wore only the insignia of the half-winged skull and wishbones. "YOU HAVEN'T EVEN LEARNED TO FLY PROPERLY!" His voice lowered to a snarl. "From where did you get the Cameracraft, may I ask?"

"I stole it from Artless . . . but I . . ."

Eraser's anger hit an all-time high. "YOOOU WHAAAT?"

"But I mu. . ."

"Don't but!" interrupted Eraser.

"But I m. . .must t. . .tell. . ."

"DON'T BUT! DON'T BUUUT!" Eraser signalled to an Eradicator standing beside him. "PUT THIS WET SOAK IN COLLAGE!"

A powerful whirlwind of multicoloured light

suddenly tore through the cavern, disappearing into the Collage wall like bath-water rushing at a ridiculous speed down a plug-hole. Taken completely by surprise, Eraser, Soaking Wet and the rest of the Eradicators were scattered all over the place.

The twins had also been given the fright of their lives, but it soon turned to joy as the Beamsurfer set down, close by, inside the Collage wall.

Eraser gazed in total disbelief as he saw the twins greet Zag and Eggbert. "Got you! Got you! I'm not sure how! AND I don't care! Because I've GOT YOU!" he shouted, bouncing around like a demented jumping-bean. "I am ERASER," he bawled out to his Eradicators. "NOBODY fools around with ERASER THE TERRIB. . ."

He suddenly stopped in his tracks. Everyone was paying attention to something else and not him. Eraser froze in shock at the sight of Astral being introduced to the twins. To add insult to injury, Astral then stood looking out from the wall with a big grin on his face, holding up the Orb like a champion World Cup footballer.

"Did he shout something at you then, Astral?" laughed Eggbert, watching Eraser's ugly facial grimaces rippling at the angry boil.

"Just as well we can't hear him," said Zag with a grin, ushering Lucy and William aboard the Beamsurfer.

"Have you figured a way out of here yet?" asked Astral. "We need to get him while he is in the cavern."

"Climb aboard," Zag called out, while thinking to himself, "This time I must make sure I don't overshoot the landing."

Zag took control and set the monitors. "The painting brush can't paint on something that is nothing," he said out loud, twiddling at the joystick, "but all pictures absorb and reflect light." He pushed some flashing buttons. "And where there's light, there's beams. . ."

A powerful whirlwind of multicoloured light suddenly tore into the cavern, appearing out of the Collage wall like bath-water rushing back up a plug-

-hole at a ridiculous speed. Once again, taken completely by surprise, Eraser and his Eradicators were scattered all over the place as the Beamsurfer landed on the cavern floor. The door of the craft flew open.

"ERADICATE THEM!" shouted Eraser, wobbling to his feet.

The Eradicators rushed towards the Beamsurfer. Zag pointed the painting brush and in a flash of light they were encapsulated in a huge block of ice. But Eraser was already making his getaway up the steps to Lucy's tunnel. Zag pointed the brush again. In a flash the top half of the steps did a U-turn from the tunnel and Eraser found himself running back towards them. Like lightning, Eggbert flew at Eraser, knocking him to the floor.

With one tug of his talon, he wrenched the Stone of Genius away from Eraser's scrawny neck. In desperation, Eraser shouted to the crew on the *Sea Err* to help, but not one of them moved to his aid.

As Astral put out his hand to receive the Stone from Eggbert, he noted some hesitancy. "You've really got to trust me now, Eggbert," he said.

Zag nodded approvingly.

"And what about Eggna, Flewy and Legs?" asked Eggbert, as he released the stone.

"They will be restored, along with the true inhabitants of this island," replied Astral.

"When?" asked Eggbert eagerly.

Astral touched Eggbert's wing and with an understanding smile said, "We must be outside of this cavern. You'll soon see why. But first we must deal with Eraser and his Eradicators."

One by one, Zag released the wet and shivering Eradicators from the huge block of ice. They were in no fit state to offer any resistance.

Astral called over the smiling crew members of the *Sea Err*, instructing them to put the Eradicators in the hold, where they would have to await their fate.

"Are you sure about this?" asked Zag.

"That's a bit risky," said William.

"I'd have thought so," said Lucy.

Astral smiled and spoke to Eggbert. "Could you take Eraser aboard the galleon while I explain?"

"My pleasure," said Eggbert, grabbing Eraser firmly by the scruff of the neck. "Hope ya can find a place to start," he laughed, taking his evil prisoner away.

"Eraser was once a Defender of the Orb, like me," said Astral. "He captained a team of Eradicators, whose task was to obliterate bad and harmful ideas. He conceitedly thought he was far too gifted and creative to be a Defender. Against the Master's will, he sent his inferior ideas into the Galaxy, hoping to dominate really creative minds. Eraser's ideas were so awful, he made no impression at all."

"Bet that put him in a bad mood," Lucy said, laughing.

"Hopping mad," said Astral, chuckling. "It's funny now, but it was far too serious to laugh at then."

"So what happened next?" asked William.

"Becoming so evil with jealousy, he convinced his Eradicators of the power he could give them by stealing the Orb. The Defenders who refused to join him were taken hostage. Then he set out to destroy all forms of creativity other than his own."

"What happened to those Defenders?" asked Lucy.

"Eraser forced them to be the crew on the *Sea Err*, so now you know why I trust them."

"Eggbert is ready," said Zag, seeing the great eagle's wing urging them aboard.

Astral put his arms around Lucy and William as they walked towards the *Sea Err*. "You are now going to experience some wonderful things as well as being reunited with your friends." He smiled at Zag. "You too, my good friend."

"What about the Beamsurfer?" said Zag.

"That is easily sorted out," replied Astral. "It's the least I can do."

"In that case, let's get back outside and see if the *Mobsea Dick* has sailed around," said Zag, grinning at the thought of it.

The Brilliant Night

The *Sea Err* surfaced between the Carrier and the now present *Mobsea Dick*. The real night sky had set in for the first time in a very long while, looking like a brilliant fireworks display of unbelievable proportions.

The handful of crew left aboard the Carrier had not been puzzled by the arrival of the gleaming *Mobsea Dick*. Extraordinary happenings on Blot were far more usual than the mere ordinary.

Awoo flew ahead of the Mogsters, leaving them to row the short distance to the *Sea Err*. He landed on board and found Zag and the others deciding what to do about the ditched Cameracraft drifting lamely close by.

"What now, old chap?" said Awoo, perching on the rail next to Zag.

"Good to see you," said Zag with a smile, "although you do look a bit green."

"Hey, pal, did ya enjoy yar trip?" cried Eggbert,

breaking off from the decision-making process.

"Those Mogsters are crazy. I spent most of my time going around in circles, having to listen to a poem Catpone's written to woo back Legs."

"I thought you did all the wooing," said William, making everybody chuckle.

Awoo didn't find it that amusing and prompted Zag to get back to business.

"I think we should get a line attached to the Cameracraft," said Zag, concerned that it didn't drift into the galleons.

"Okay," said Astral, "then we can decide what to do with it once we have released everybody from Collage."

Zag reached into his Thingummajacket, pulled out his Frisberang and handed it to Eggbert. "Do you reckon you could you attach this securely to the Cameracraft?"

The line reeled out smoothly as Zag held on to the Frisberang and Eggbert flew it across to the Cameracraft. Zag clipped a matchbox-sized unit into the Frisberang. With his special clamp, he fixed the Frisberang to a sturdy capstan, then pressed a button. The small but very powerful motor hauled the craft gently alongside the *Sea Err*.

Lucy and William, still astonished at how the galleon had turned into a submarine, stood wondering what amazing things would happen next.

"This has been fantastic," said William.

"It is now, and it will be even better when Flewy and Legs are released," Lucy said, as Eggbert returned to the poop-deck.

"And Eggna," said William.

"Uh . . . hey . . . fellas, FELLAS! Da ya wanna hear my piece of poultry I've dun for Legs?" shouted Catpone, clambering up the poop-deck steps. "Uh . . . I've evun mesmowized it."

"Memorized it, boss," Gutrumble corrected.

Spooky followed behind them, poking a paw-like finger down his throat.

Eggbert grinned nervously. "I think everyone is aboard now."

Astral called for everybody's attention. "Now it is time to release all our friends from Collage and return this island to the Rutilans, its rightful inhabitants."

Everybody applauded enthusiastically.

"It is very important that the World of Creativity has not one single remnant of a Blot on its map. Therefore, under the strict control of my Defenders and by the power of the Orb, I have decided that the Eradicators will help the Rutilans to restore this island, thus allowing them to once more put the glow into the sunset."

"What about dat cweep Ewaser?" Gutrumble asked.

"I will take him to face the Master, who will punish him." Astral carefully opened the Orb. For a moment, the brilliance of the light from the Stones of Skill, Inspiration and Imagination blinded the eyes of all those who were watching. "HAPPY LANDINGS, EVERYONE," he called out, then locked the Stone of Genius into the other stones.

Without warning, the volcanic mountain of Collage exploded into life. From it gushed a fountain of fluorescent red, blue and green. Bright sparkling images of all forms and shapes surged high into the sky. Some rained softly on the island, while others fell delicately into the sea.

Legs landed gently on the deck beside Catpone, who in all the excitement had at that very moment forgotten his poem.

"NOT THE CATS!" shrieked Flewy, as he landed next to Gutrumble, then dashed behind a welcoming Zag for cover.

The volcano gushed as others were released and took off towards the heavens in a burst of glittering, fiery energy, leaving behind a brilliant silvery cloud. Suddenly all became calm. There was a long silence and then out of the cloud flew a lone eagle.

"Go on, Eggbert," said Zag, "this is the

moment you have waited for."

Without any further encouragement, Eggbert took off to meet Eggna in the illuminated sky. For a short while they soared together in a manner that no stunt pilot could ever hope to achieve.

"Spectacular," gasped William.

"That's so romantic," drooled Lucy.

"Hey . . . uh, Legs, I've evun mesmowized some poultry for ya," said Catpone, anxious to recite his poem.

"Ya couldn't mesmowize a wabbit, ya wimp," said Legs, sticking her "pwitty" nose in the air. "And getta new suit, ya look stoopid dwessed in pink."

Awoo was taking great pleasure in half-scaring Flewy to death by saying how much Gutrumble loved him and was looking forward to a kiss.

Suddenly, in the midst of all, the Cameracraft unexpectedly roared into life. The shouting and rushing about from some of the Defenders signalled that Eraser the Terrible had escaped. Having taken advantage of the huge distraction, he had managed to free his spindly wrists from his bonds.

The Frisberang's line reeled out furiously as the still-attached Cameracraft took off towards the reef. Soon the line had reeled its course, but it still held on to the craft firmly, like a huge kite in the sky.

The Defenders desperately tried to manoeuvre

the large flash-gun mounted on the quarter-deck, but the gleaming *Mobsea Dick* was partially blocking their aim.

"DON'T SHOOT!" shouted Astral, realizing the danger of everybody on the *Sea Err* being caught in the reflection.

They watched helplessly as the Cameracraft surged with a desperate thrust of power. With a piercing twang, the line snapped, making Eraser and the craft plummet in an explosion of light into the sea just beyond the reef.

For a moment everyone stood dumbfounded, then all except Zag broke into rapturous applause.

"I hope the sea is very deep out there," said Zag with concern.

"Bottomless," said Gutrumble, bent over the rail and peering out to sea.

Spooky glanced at Gutrumble's ample rear. "Yeah, an' don' I wish."

Zag stood next to Astral. "Do you think Eraser survived?"

"It's very deep. If he did, the Lurks would get him," said Astral.

"Lurks?" asked Zag.

"Foul creatures that lurk in the depths, living off Eraser's pollution. Ironically, if he has survived, Eraser will probably be their final meal."

"Sounds nasty," said Zag. "Talking of which, how did you get involved with Eraser?"

"I couldn't prevent him stealing the Orb even though I was loyal to the Master. I joined him, hoping that I could retrieve it."

"Well, I guess the job is done," said Zag,

watching with pleasure as Eggbert and Eggna landed nearby and began to cuddle each other.

Astral grinned handsomely and called everybody together for one last time.

"Oh, no!" said Flewy impatiently. "Why can't things happen without speeches?"

"Behave!" Lucy scolded.

Astral spoke. "You have all seen what devastation can be caused if evil holds the Orb of Brilliance. Without the help of our friends, we would not be here now. Occasionally, not often, someone special, like Zagwitz, trustworthy without question, is bestowed with extra special gifts. And I would like to thank him." Astral paused and smiled at Zag, while they all applauded.

Zag lifted his fez and scratched his head. "And thanks to all of you," he said, a touch embarrassed at all the attention being paid to him.

"No! You tell them," William whispered to Lucy, thinking it more appropriate.

"William and I thought instead of calling it Blot, let's rename it Radiant Island," Lucy suggested.

"The Island of Radiance. What a terrific idea," said Astral.

"And you can visit Eggbert and me whenever you wish," said Eggna.

"Uh . . . and us as well, cos we're weally, uh

. . . hospital," said Catpone.

"Hospitable," corrected Gutrumble.

"Yeah, and change your diet," said Flewy.

"Okay, fwom now on no more wats or burdies," Gutrumble promised. "I'll eat fish now der water's good."

Zag looked at Flewy. "Well, I guess it is time for us all to go home."

"Where would you like the Beamsurfer to be put?" asked Astral.

"The twins' back garden would be ideal, if you would be so kind," said Zag.

"Then that is where it will be, my friend," said Astral. He closed the Orb and held it up in the air in the palm of his hand, saying, "Protect within each fiery stone locked as one, each never alone."

The Orb shone brighter and brighter as it spun above his hand, rising into the sky and quickly growing bigger and bigger until it was the size of two tennis courts. A pathway of light came from its brilliance and touched the Sea Err. Astral walked to the edge of the light and beckoned Zag, Flewy, Awoo and the twins to follow. "This is the quick way home for you as well as me. What is more, I can make sure that all of you arrive safely." He smiled.

They were all happy to go home, but also sad in having to leave Eggbert, Eggna, Legs and the Mogster crew.

"Aw, shucks, I wish I 'adn't bin so wotten to Flewy, Awoo and dose kids," said Gutrumble, waving to them, as he watched them enter the light and disappear into the Orb.

It spun for a moment longer and then they were gone.

Well, Would You Believe It!

". . . Here is the eight o'clock news. During last night Big Ben, the Statue of Liberty, the Eiffel Tower, the Sydney Opera House, the pyramids and all works of art returned to normal. Witnesses say that these events were preceded by a glowing ball of blinding white light. This welcome news is still baffling the scientists, who for the moment are . . ."

"Fantastic!" said Mike. "Did you hear that?"

"Great news," said Zag, helping to lay the kitchen table for breakfast.

"Morning," said Lucy, wandering into the kitchen.

"Morning," said William, as the others followed behind him.

"You all look very bleary-eyed this morning," said Mike.

"Looks like we have an additional guest," said Sally-Anne, seeing Awoo and about to serve up breakfast. "Just arrived?"

"His brain is still on its way," muttered Flewy.

"Ahem." Awoo coughed, thinking this was not the time or place to argue with a smelly, overblown sea duck.

"Well, I hope you're all up to solving the mystery of the sea-chest," said Mike, sitting down at the table. "Mum has said she'll help after breakfast."

The kitchen filled with laughter.

"Sorry," said Zag. "I think I had better try and explain."

The laughter continued for some time, as did the explanation, but eventually it was time for Zag, Awoo and Flewy to go back to the barn. The twins, with their mum and dad, walked with them to the Beamsurfer, which was in the garden as Astral had promised.

Zag, Flewy and Awoo said their goodbyes and boarded the Beamsurfer.

"How did Mike's trawler pass through the *Sea Err* ?" Awoo asked.

"It hit the *Sea Err* as it was dematerializing back to Blot," answered Zag, as he set the co-ordinates. "Safety-belts on, please."

"Then why didn't the sea-chest disappear?" asked Flewy.

"It fell overboard before that process started."

Awoo looked none the wiser as Zag noticed a

handwritten Post-it note stuck on the screen. He read it out to Flewy and Awoo.

Dear Zag,

I hope you don't mind but I have added some modifications to your Beamsurfer, some of which you must keep secret for others to discover in the future. Some you will find to be a lot of fun.
Love and a big thank-you to you all,
Astral, Eggna and Eggbert.

PS: We and the Orb of Brilliance are never far away for those who wish to seek us.

"Well, would you believe it!" said Zag.

"Yes, I would," said Flewy, looking concerned. "So please don't try any of them on the way back home."

"I second that," said Awoo.

"Don't worry. I promise I won't," said Zag, with a big hearty laugh. "I will leave that for some other time."

And with that they surfed the homeward beam.

KAREN WALLACE

Raspberries
on the
Yangtze

"Can a book be funny, perceptive, moving and
utterly absorbing at one and the same time?
This one can. Brilliant.
A *'Swallows and Amazons'* for the 21st century."

Michael Morpurgo

£7.99 · ISBN: 0 689 82796 2